TONY CORREIA

JAMES LORIMER & COMPANY LTD., PUBLISHERS
TORONTO

James Lorimer & Company Ltd., Publishers acknowledges funding support
from the Ontario Arts Council (OAC), an agency of the Government
of Ontario. We acknowledge the support of the Canada Council for the
Arts, which last year invested $153 million to bring the arts to Canadians
throughout the country. This project has been made possible in part by the
Government of Canada and with the support of Ontario Creates.

Cover design: Tyler Cleroux
Cover image: Shutterstock

Library and Archives Canada Cataloguing in Publication (Paperback)

Title: Walk this way / Tony Correia.
Names: Correia, Tony, author.
Series: RealLove.
Description: Series statement: Real love
Identifiers: Canadiana (print) 20210210613 | Canadiana (ebook) 2021021063X
    | ISBN 9781459416314 (softcover) | ISBN 9781459416321 (EPUB)
Classification: LCC PS8605.O768 W35 2021 | DDC jC813/.6—dc23

Published by: Distributed in Canada by: Distributed in the US by:
James Lorimer &   Formac Lorimer Books   Lerner Publisher Services
Company Ltd., Publishers   5502 Atlantic Street   241 1st Ave. N.
117 Peter Street, Suite 304 Halifax, NS, Canada   Minneapolis, MN, USA
Toronto, ON, Canada   B3H 1G4   55401
M5V 0M3   www.lernerbooks.com
www.lorimer.ca

Printed and bound in Canada.
Manufactured by Friesens Corporation in Altona, Manitoba,
Canada in June 2021.
Job #277242

For Bill Monroe.

01 Ghosted

I WALK INTO THE RESTAURANT feeling like a million bucks. You could bounce a quarter off my ass in my skinny jeans. I haven't been able to feel my balls since I got off the SkyTrain. They might be numb. The UnderArmour shirt I "borrowed" from my brother Ed is bringing much needed definition to my chest and shoulders. If I didn't know better, I'd swear I worked out. My face has that desired Instagram filter glow. There's a chance I may have single-handedly destroyed a small rainforest achieving this look. But beauty takes no prisoners. If this date goes as planned, I promise to make it up to Mother Earth.

The restaurant is packed with rugged-looking men and women. I'm seeing lots of ballcaps and gym bags. There's an active game of darts happening. And here I was thinking people only played competitive darts on TV. A posse of pool players are analyzing the balls on the table like they're landing a rover on Mars. Forty-inch monitors light up the restaurant with baseball, football and hockey games. When Randall described the Dugout as a place where "sporty" gays go, I pictured yoga pants and Abercrombie & Fitch varsity shirts, not actual sports. The only gay thing about the place is the portrait of Freddy Mercury.

"For how many?" the musclebound host asks me.

"Joshua!"

I look in the direction of my name and see a hand waving above the ballcaps.

"I found my date, thanks," I tell the host.

My first date ever. With Randall, the hottest gay

guy at school, no less. If my friends could see me now, they would totally judge me. My best friend Kara never had time for Randall because he's a jock. She resents him more now that he came out of the closet a couple of weeks ago. Kara told me girls were literally crying in the bathroom when they heard the news that he's gay. I always had my suspicions. Seriously, how many straight guys wear T-shirts cut off at the midriff?

I squeeze through chair backs and step over backpacks to get to Randall. It's like a locker room with table service. I trip on a curling broom, and almost fall flat on my face before Randall catches me.

"I didn't plan that, I swear," I tell him.

Randall props me back up on my feet. He's a good inch taller than me. He has perfect black Superman hair, a sculpted nose that looks like it's never caught cold and a cleft in his chin I want to rest all my hopes and dreams in. I still can't believe he said yes when I asked him to go on a date with me.

"Have a seat," Randall says. "Unless you want to eat standing up."

I snort-laugh, then try to cover it up by pretending to have a coughing fit.

"Have some water," Randall says, offering me the glass in front of him. I take a sip and wave away my fake coughing spasm like it's nothing. Which it is.

"Nice place," I lie.

"It's one of the few gay places that serves minors. This is where I would come when I was still coming to terms with being gay. Did you have any trouble finding it?"

"Siri led me right here."

"I hope you didn't mind taking the SkyTrain from New West. I would have offered to drive you, but I had to take my sister to swim practice."

"It's all good." Another lie. If he was going to make me come all the way downtown from the burbs, the least he could have done is given me a lift. But that cleft in his chin, it does things to me.

Our waiter has a body like John Cena and a voice like Ross Matthews. Randall already knows what he wants to eat. I open the menu and point to the first thing under fifteen dollars. A club sandwich.

"I have to be honest," Randall says. "You're not really my type. I prefer more masculine, straight-acting guys. But you have some nice definition going on there. And I was impressed that you had the nerve to ask me out on a date. That took balls."

"When I know what I want, I go after it," I say. I'm trying to sound cooler than I really am.

"You're like your brother Ed when he chases the puck playing hockey. I much preferred being on his team than playing against him in house league. He still plays, doesn't he?"

"He's trying to get into Juniors. He's determined to play for Team Canada."

"You look athletic for a thin guy," Randall says, changing the subject. "What do you bench press?"

"Do push-ups count?"

"You don't lift weights?"

"No, but I look after my figure. I have to if I plan on performing at Poodles."

"What's Poodles?"

"The drag cabaret up the street from here. Haven't you seen me on IG? I'm Siri Alexa. I have ten thousand followers." I pull my phone out of my pocket and start scrolling through my photo stream.

"You're a drag queen?"

"Not in real life. But I will be. I make all my own costumes. I can paint my face in my sleep."

"You never said you were a drag queen."

"I'm more of a Look Queen. You can't call yourself a drag queen until you've performed in front of a live audience." I hear the legs of Randall's chair scrape across the floor as they are pushed back from the table. "Where are you going?"

Randall is putting on his jacket. He leaves the table without saying goodbye. The waiter returns with our food and puts it down in front of me.

"I don't have enough money to pay for all this," I tell him.

"Honey, I saw the whole thing," the waiter lisps. "This is on the house."

"Can I have it to go?" I ask sheepishly.

At least I can feel my balls again. They're stuck in my throat.

02 The Wonder Twins

WHEN THE GOING GETS TOUGH, the tough do drag. Instead of drowning my sorrows in a pint of Ernest Ice Cream, I've invited the Wonder Twins, Kara and Chris, over to help me with a lip-sync video. Kara is an Asian dyke, and Chris is her Goth twin brother. We met at a pep rally in grade nine. Like me, they were trying to distance themselves from the enthusiastic student body. We've been thick as thieves ever since.

"For someone with so much going for him, you

sure keep a lot of secrets," Chris says, after I tell the twins about my date.

"Whatever possessed you to ask Randall out?" Kara asks. "You knew he was a jerk before he came out."

"This is exactly why I didn't tell you," I say.

"Randall is the kind of guy you meet on Grindr," Chris says. "And you know what the guys on there are like: No fats, no femmes, no Asians."

"It was an impulse decision," I tell them. "I had just topped ten thousand followers on Insta. I felt invincible and I went for it without thinking. It was a real rush."

"Down the toilet," Kara says.

"He was probably using you to get to your brother," Chris says.

"Both of you are doing wonders for my self-esteem," I say.

"You are the most talented person I know," says Kara. "You can draw, you can sew and you can repair anything. You can do better than Randall."

Up to now, Siri Alexa's Instagram feed has been filled with selfies of me modelling clothes I've designed and made myself. But social media is crawling with Look Queens. Real divas *perform* on a stage. My plan is to use this video as a calling card. With any luck, I'll be performing at Poodles in no time. I position myself in front of the tripod.

"How do I look?" I ask Chris, who is looking at me through the camera on my phone. "Can you see my entire body in the frame?"

"As long as you don't move your hands, feet or head," Chris says.

The door opens and my brother Ed tromps into the apartment, dragging his hockey bag behind him. He sees me in drag, my wig blowing in the wind from the fan that Kara is pointing toward my face.

"Mom!" Ed shouts to the kitchen. "Josh is doing drag in the living room again."

"Stop stirring the turd, Ed!" Mom shouts back. Mom has no patience for Ed's complaints ever since my dad moved in with her best friend. Or as Mom calls her, "That Bitch Becky."

Ed goes into our room and shuts the door behind him.

"Cue the music, Kara." I turn my back to the camera, take a deep breath, and channel my inner Carly Rae Jepsen. I point to Kara, and say, "Hit it!"

I spin around dramatically and start mouthing the words to "Party for One."

THUMP! THUMP! THUMP!

"Cut!" I shout.

"What's that?" Kara asks.

"Bill, the bitchy old queen who lives downstairs," I say. "He bangs on the ceiling if I sigh too loud. Turn down the volume or we'll never get through this take."

We start the song over from the beginning. I smile coyly at the camera, pushing my fake boobs together to make them look bigger. I start to feel self-conscious and silly dancing in front of the camera for the Wonder Twins. Then I get tongue-tied during the chorus. I try to cover it up by moving my head back and forth to distract attention from my lips. This is harder than I thought it was going to be. I push through to the end of the song, dancing and smiling, trying to show my imaginary audience a good time. I'm out of breath when the song ends. I feel good.

"What did you think?" I ask Kara and Chris.

They're silent, like when they're solving a math problem.

"Why don't you see for yourself," Chris says.

I join the Wonder Twins behind the tripod. Chris presses Play. I can't take my eyes off myself. It's a hundred times better than what I pictured in my head.

"I am awesome," I say.

"Are your eyes tone deaf?" Kara says.

"It's not bad for the first time," I say.

"You're wearing flats," Chris says.

"I don't know how to walk in heels," I say.

"And when you dance, your dress looks like a bird trying to fly for the first time," says Kara.

"What do you know?" I snap. "You haven't worn a dress since your First Communion."

"I know when a woman is rocking a dress," she says.

"People love my drag on Instagram," I say.

"Because they don't know you," Chris says.

"Thanks!" I say.

"What he means is, Carly Rae Jepsen isn't you," Kara says. "Why aren't you doing Amy Winehouse? You love Amy Winehouse!"

"No one our age knows who she is," I say.

"How many people our age know who Carly Rae Jepsen is?" says Chris.

"She just put out an album a couple of years ago!" I say.

"I like Carly Rae Jepsen, too," Kara says. "But you're too arty to be a pop princess."

"It would take three wigs to create one of Amy Winehouse's hairstyles," I say. "And she has all those tattoos . . ."

"You don't have to *be* her," Chris says. "Just draw your inspiration *from* her."

"The Josh I know and love is fearless," Kara says. "But the woman in that video looks like a girl who's embarrassed about her boobs."

"I'm not feeling so fearless now," I say.

"What you need is a drag mother to help you channel your inner Amy Winehouse," Chris says. "And to teach you how to walk in heels."

"Chris is right," Kara says. "You've spent so much time alone in your room reading fashion magazines and watching YouTube videos on drag, you don't know how to be a drag queen in real life. A drag mother will put you through your paces."

We shoot the video a couple more times. Watching the playback, I totally see what the Wonder Twins are talking about. This whole time, I thought I was a drag prodigy, when I'm actually a bottom feeder. In one day, I get ghosted for doing drag and find out I was never really good at it to begin with.

How can this day get any worse? And where am I going to find a drag mother in suburbs?

THUMP! THUMP! THUMP!

03 Hockey Night in Canada

I'M ON A ZOOM CALL in the living room with Kara and Chris, trying to figure out a stupid math equation. I hate math. Kara and Chris are math geniuses. They watch me from their spot on a tablet while I try solving the equation on my laptop.

"Just tell me the answer," I say.

"It's more fun watching you torture yourself," Chris says.

"When did Goths become so bitchy?" I say to

the tablet.

"All Goths are bitchy," Kara says. "It's because they're over everything."

Ed comes out of the bathroom wearing his robe. He is freshly showered and smelling of Axe body spray. What is it with straight guys and Axe body spray? Why not just spray yourself with bug repellent?

"Hey, loser," he says. "Want to go to a Vancouver Giants hockey game with me and a buddy from work? I have an extra ticket."

Ed works part-time delivering beds for Dreamland, the mattress store at Metrotown shopping centre. If his co-workers are anything like his buddies at school, the only thing we'll have in common is that we require air and water to survive. I don't mind hockey. I just can't stand all the toxic masculinity in the bleachers.

"When have I ever wanted to go to a hockey game?" I say, rolling my eyes like Chris does whenever he opens his mouth.

"I was being nice," Ed says. "If you would rather stay here and play dress up, then suit yourself."

Ed goes into our bedroom to get dressed. I feel like a jerk for shooting him down the way I did. We get along well, even though we're constantly ribbing each other. We've both been known to take things too far.

"Can we get back to work here?" Kara asks from the tablet.

The analog phone on the wall rings. It must be Ed's work buddy.

"Just a second, someone's here," I say, getting up.

I buzz Ed's friend into the building. My butt hasn't even warmed my seat when I hear the knock at the door.

"Can you get that, Joshy?" Ed shouts from our room. Ed still talks to me like I'm five, even though he's only a year older and a grade ahead of me.

"You're doing this on purpose!" Kara shouts from the tablet.

"Sorry," I say to the twins.

I run to get the door as quick as I can. I take a step back when I see who is on the other side. His face is all smiles, laugh lines and freckles. His eyes are like crystal balls. I have to stop myself from running my fingers through his curly red hair. And he doesn't smell like Axe body spray.

"Is Ed here?" he asks.

"Yes! Come on in," I say, holding the door open for him. "I'm Josh, Ed's brother."

"You should really ask who it is before you let someone into the building," he says, entering the apartment. "There are a lot of crazy people out there posing as Amazon delivery guys. I'm Ivan, by the way."

"You certainly are," I say, not taking my eyes off him.

"Sorry?"

"Nothing."

I can hear Kara and Chris shouting at me from the tablet. I go over to the dining room table and turn the tablet off without saying goodbye.

"Cool couch," Ivan says.

"I re-upholstered it myself," I say.

"Get out of town!"

"I'm really good with fabrics," I say. "Everything you need to know is on YouTube."

"Hey, Ivan," Ed says, coming from our room wearing a Canucks jersey.

"Your brother said he re-upholstered that couch," Ivan says in disbelief.

"He did," Ed says. "He pissed off our downstairs neighbour with the racket he made doing it."

"That's so awesome!" Ivan says, like I just pulled a quarter from behind his ear. His enthusiasm is contagious. I've never met anyone this upbeat who I didn't want to smother with a pillow.

"Is that extra hockey ticket still up for grabs?" I ask Ed.

"I tore it up into a million pieces," Ed says. "Of course the ticket is up for grabs."

I have no idea what I'm doing. I could be setting myself up for disappointment, like I did with Randall. But if someone as good-looking as Ivan is so easily impressed by some fabric I stretched over a couch, then the bar is already pretty low. I can only go up from here.

♥ ♥ ♥

I forgot how much fun going to a hockey game is. The puck is moving up and down the ice so fast I can barely keep up with it. But I'm not here to cheer for the home team. I want Ivan to notice me.

"So, what does the guy with the leg warmers do again?" I ask Ivan.

"The goalie?" Ivan says, laughing.

"You know what a goalie is, Josh," Ed says, keeping his eyes on the game. "Josh played house league for a few years and then quit. It broke my dad's heart."

"Why did you stop?" Ivan asks, his eyes still on the game.

"I hated getting up early on the weekends," I say. Ed knows this is a lie. I was picked on mercilessly. It tainted my opinion of the game. I never told my dad, though. I was too embarrassed.

"I stopped playing after I got crosschecked from behind," Ivan says. "I was out cold for, like, a minute."

"You never told me that," Ed says.

The Vancouver Giants score and the crowd is on its feet. The three of us jump up and down like we scored the goal ourselves. Without thinking, I throw my arms around Ivan's shoulders, like I would Kara and Chris. I see the look of surprise on Ivan's face and let go right away. We both look embarrassed. I can't tell if Ivan is embarrassed for me or because he enjoyed the hug as much as I did.

A fight breaks out on the ice. The benches are cleared. Gloves and sticks litter the ice, as both teams hang onto the other's jerseys so they can punch each other in the face. The fans are thirsty for blood. They're more excited about the fight than they are about the goal.

I turn my face away from the ice, like it's the scary part in a movie. I feel Ivan's hand squeeze my shoulder. "It's okay, buddy," he says into my ear. His voice soothes me, and he rubs my back until the fight is over and the game resumes.

04 Miss Bill

I HAVE THE APARTMENT to myself. Mom is out making extra cash driving Uber. Ed is playing hockey with his friends. I wonder if Ivan is with him. Maybe Ed will bring Ivan around to the apartment again tonight. On second thought, I don't want Ivan to see me in drag.

I'm taking Kara and Chris's advice and painting my face to look like Amy Winehouse. I'm struggling with her Egyptian eyeliner. I look more eighties Goth than sixties Goddess. I grab my biggest wig and try to shape it into a beehive with so much hairspray I nearly pass out from the fumes. I throw a tank top over a black bra, put on a pleather mini-skirt I found for five dollars at Value Village and check my look in the mirror. Not bad if I say so myself. And now for the hard part. Performing as Amy Winehouse.

"Hey, Siri," I say to my phone. "Play 'Rehab' by Amy Winehouse."

The song plays on the Bluetooth speaker. I start mouthing the words to my reflection in the mirror. I can already tell it's all wrong.

THUMP! THUMP! THUMP!

I stomp on the floor with my foot, turn up the volume and keep on performing. The music is so loud I don't hear the pounding on the door until the song is over.

I go to the door and put my eye to the peephole. A withered face with white hair is staring back at me. I throw open the door, filled with piss and vinegar. Our downstairs neighbour already has his mouth open ready to lay into me. He sees me in my drag and doubles over laughing.

"Can I help you with something, Bill?" I ask.

"That's *Miss* Bill to you," he says. "And I've seen undercover cops do better drag than you."

"You climbed a flight of stairs to tell me that?"

"Turn down your music! I can't hear *Coronation Street*." Miss Bill plants his cane and turns to leave.

"I'm changing my look," I say to him. "I'm usually more polished than this."

Miss Bill stops, leans on his cane and looks me over from head to toe.

"Let me guess. You're auditioning for one of those reality shows," Miss Bill says, pronouncing 'reality' like the Queen of England. "When I was coming up in the drag scene, I had to dodge cops and beer bottles to become a star. Now all you need is a phone."

"You were a *drag* queen?" I say, following him down the hall.

"*Were*? I'm still a drag queen! Now turn down your music and let me go back to my stories." Miss Bill flips an imaginary scarf over his shoulder, sticks his nose in the air, and continues down the hall.

"Wait!" I say following him down the stairs.

"What now?"

"Will you be my drag mother?"

Miss Bill stops on the stairs and looks back up at me. "No!"

I refuse to take no for an answer. I follow him to his apartment door.

"What do you think you're doing?" he asks.

"Why won't you be my drag mother?"

"Who do I look like? Your grandmother?"

"You have the same wig."

Miss Bill gasps and puts a hand to his throat like he's been accused of murder. An evil grin spreads from cheek to cheek. "You can come in," he says. "But don't touch anything."

Miss Bill's living room is lit with antique lamps with scarves draped over them. There's a bearskin rug with its head attached and velvet furniture that looks like it came from a castle. Against one wall is a bookcase filled with foam heads adorned with wigs, crowns and necklaces. Another wall is decorated with posters for the Great Pretenders.

I point to one of the four drag queens on the poster and ask, "Is that you?"

"Certainly is. I did a better Judy Garland than Judy Garland."

"Who's Judy Garland?"

"Wash your mouth!" Miss Bill says. "Even you must have seen *The Wizard of Oz.*"

"You mean Dorothy?"

"Dorothy was only the beginning. Without Judy, there would be no Cher, no Madonna . . ."

"No Gaga?" I say.

"Are you having a stroke?"

"This is why I need you to be my drag mother. I need someone to explain who Judy Garland and Cher are."

"You don't know who Cher is?" Bill points to the door. "Get out!"

"I was kidding. I wanted to see how upset you would get."

"While I can appreciate a queen who presses buttons, I'm too old to be a drag mother again.

I'm retired. Don't you have BoobTube or whatever it is to show you everything you need to know?"

"I can do the make-up and the hair. It's the performing I need help with."

"My point exactly. A drag mother is supposed to put you in drag for the first time. Your cherry is popped."

"Please. I need to prove to myself and everyone in the world that I can do this."

"You do have a flair for melodrama. That's always a sign of a good drag queen," Miss Bill says. He looks me over one more time. "You look like you fell off a truck. Fine, I'll do it out of pity. But you have to promise to trust my judgement."

"You're a life saver," I say, going to give him a hug. Miss Bill backs way, putting his hands in front of him.

"We'll have none of that," Miss Bill says. "I have a reputation to uphold. Now get out of my apartment. TTFN!"

"Don't you mean TTYL?"

"TTFN. Ta-Ta For Now. What are you? A caveman?"

I go back to our apartment to de-drag, but the door is locked. I bang my head against it. I have no idea what time Ed or my mom are coming home. Magically, the door opens from the other side. Ed is standing there in a T-shirt and boxers.

"Mom!" Ed shouts over his shoulder. "Joshua is doing drag in the hallway."

The joke is on him. Mom isn't home.

05 The Hockey Type

I KEEP MYSELF in make-up and dresses by doing gig work for a food delivery app. It's not bad as far as part-time jobs go. I can work as much or as little as I want. The pay sucks. I have to hustle my bike all around town to make any serious coin. And there was that time I delivered a meal to Mr. Ronson, my English teacher. He was obviously stoned and on a date when he answered the door. I got a ten-dollar cash tip out of that delivery.

It's been getting harder and harder to sign onto the app now that it's getting colder and darker out. Miss Bill wants to take me out shopping for heels on the weekend. I don't want to spend all the money I've saved on women's shoes. But I don't want to break my neck on a cheap pair of heels either.

I don't hesitate to pick up a delivery from the Greek restaurant not far from my house. I pedal my bike to a house near Moody Park. I've started closing my eyes and holding my breath before the door opens ever since that delivery to Mr. Ronson. I've delivered food to a couple of people from school. They either pretend not to recognize me or feel sorry for me. Whatever. One day when I'm a superstar they'll tell their friends about the time I delivered a Big Mac to them when they were too high to go to McDonald's.

"Joshua?"

I open my eyes and see Ivan standing in the doorway. He's wearing sweatpants and a BC Lions jersey. He looks even hotter than he did at the hockey game.

"Hey, Ivan," I say, holding up his food. "Dinner is here!"

"Are you hungry? I have the place to myself. My parents are at the movies."

I should really be earning money for those heels. But when am I going to get another chance to be alone with Ivan?

"Sure," I say. "Let me sign out of the app."

I hand Ivan his food and follow him to the kitchen. He sets two places for us at the kitchen island. He opens the take-out container and distributes the lamb kebabs, rice and Greek salad between our plates. It feels like we're living together.

"I'm surprised you're not in front of your computer playing video games or watching porn," I say, testing the waters. I need to see if I can suss out if he's gay or not.

"What makes you think that?"

"Because you're a guy and you're friends with my brother."

"Would it surprise you to learn that I enjoy

musicals?" Ivan says.

"You're just pulling my leg," I say. I try not to come across as too interested by this revelation.

"I like *Hamilton*."

"Everyone likes *Hamilton*. Talk to me when you've seen *Rent*."

"I've seen *Rent*. I didn't like it."

"Wash your mouth!"

"I just think people should pay their rent."

"So, you're a capitalist."

"I believe in paying your dues," he says. Ivan touches my chin. "You had rice on your face."

Did I really? Or did he just want to touch my face? Am I going to spend the rest of the evening examining everything he says and every move he makes? Probably.

"I was really surprised when Ed said you played hockey," Ivan says.

"Why?"

I can see Ivan searching for a polite way to say that I'm gay AF.

"You don't seem like the hockey type," he finally says.

"I'll have you know that I'm every bit as competitive as my brother," I tell him. "Dad enrolled me in all the same sports as Ed. And I was good at all of them."

"So why did you stop playing? And don't give me that line about getting up early."

"It's like you said, I'm not the hockey type," I tell him. "But I practiced really hard to get my father to notice me. I can prove it."

"I have a couple of sticks and a net in the garage."

"You're on."

Ivan sets up the net in the driveway and hands me a stick. He puts an orange street-hockey ball in the centre of the driveway. We are both bent at the knees, staring each other in the eyes, our sticks across our hips. I've never looked into another boy's eyes so intently. It scares me a little, even though he's smiling.

"First person who scores ten goals wins," he says. Then he clunks my forehead with his own.

Ivan wins the faceoff. He takes the ball to the

bottom of the driveway and works his way back up, trying to get past me. It's been a while since I've played ball hockey. I'm out of practice. Ivan scores handily on the empty net. I'm surprised at how annoyed I am that I let him score.

Ivan gets two more goals before I figure out how he plays. I outshoot him a couple of times and tie up the game. We play like this for nearly an hour. Taking possession of the ball from each other. Going to the bottom of the driveway and working our way up again. The game gets a little physical, but not aggressive like when I played. It's like we're looking for an excuse to touch each other. I score the winning goal and raise my stick above my head like Sidney Crosby.

Ivan collapses on the lawn. I fall down next to him. We are both staring up at the night sky. The stars are coming out. Steam is rising from our skin. I can't remember the last time I've exercised this hard.

"You got lucky," Ivan says.

"Admit it," I say. "You got played."

Ivan raises himself up on his elbow. "You're fun

to hang out with," he says. "You're very competitive without being a jerk about it."

"You're very outgoing without being annoying about it," I say.

"Was that supposed to be a compliment?"

"Yes."

Ivan lies back on the grass. "Would it be okay if I texted you sometime?" Ivan says to the sky. "We don't have to talk on the phone or anything."

I wonder if Ivan doesn't want anyone to know that we are hanging out or if he's still coming to grips with being gay, like Randall. I take a moment to decide if I want to be the person Ivan learns how to be gay with. I've had a taste of that already and I didn't care for it very much. But I refuse to not get involved with someone because of one bad date.

"Okay," I say.

"Cool."

He gets up from the grass and offers his hand to help me up to my feet. I go get my bike and I'm about to ride away. Then I slam on the brakes.

"Do you mind not telling my brother we hung out tonight?" I ask him. "He can be a little weird sometimes."

"Sure thing," Ivan says, like he's relieved that I brought it up first.

We both have our reasons for wanting to keep this a secret from Ed. Maybe he doesn't want Ed to think he's gay. But I definitely don't want Ivan to know I do drag until I'm sure I know what this is.

06 Pink Cadillac

THE CARS BEHIND US are leaning on their horns. Every sort of homophobic slur is being yelled at us through rolled-down car windows as they drive past. I would be totally humiliated holding up traffic this way if Miss Bill's 1960 pink Cadillac didn't look like it just came off the assembly line.

"Should I get out and push?" I ask.

"Don't rush me. All it takes is one fender-bender to lose my license."

"It would have been faster to take the SkyTrain."

"But look at all the attention we're getting."

We pull into the parking lot at Metrotown. After the third lap of circling the lot, I finally say, "Will you pick a spot, already?"

"I'm looking for Doris Day parking."

"Who's Doris Day?"

"A movie star from the fifties and sixties who always found parking right in front of wherever she was going." The car screeches to a stop. "Found it! Right next to the entrance to The Bay!"

I can't remember the last time I was in a department store. The little shopping I do is online or at thrift stores. The smell of the perfume counter gives me a headache. The store shelves are crammed with useless things that are destined for landfill.

Miss Bill is in heaven. He allows himself to be sprayed with perfume and tests every skin cream and lotion. I've only known him as the angry old queen from downstairs. It's nice seeing him so happy. I watch as he examines his skin in a mirror and imagine him getting ready for a show with the Great Pretenders.

"Up the escalator, young man," Miss Bill says. "We need to find you some sensible heels."

"Wouldn't they be cheaper at Winners?"

"Trust your drag mother, darling," he says.

He heads in the direction of the sale rack like he's a drag divining rod. We are the only men looking at women's shoes. I notice a woman watching us. I feel embarrassed.

"Try these on for size," Miss Bill says, shoving a pair of heels at me.

"People are looking!" I whisper.

"Let them," he says. "I didn't go to jail in the nineteen-sixties so you could be embarrassed trying on a pair of heels in the twenty-twenties."

I take off my shoes and socks, then squeeze my feet into the heels. My legs feel wobbly when I stand up in them. I try walking and nearly fall into the shoe rack.

"How do they feel?" Miss Bill asks.

"They're killing my feet."

"But your calves look amazing."

Miss Bill knows the cashier. He gives us his staff discount. No wonder Miss Bill wanted to come here for the shoes. The shoes are fifty dollars, half what I was prepared to spend. Miss Bill pushes my hand away when I reach for my wallet.

"I didn't get to dress you up in drag your first time," he says. "Let me buy your first pair of heels."

Purchase made, we drive back to New Westminster at a snail's pace and have lunch at the Unicorn. The Unicorn is the closest thing we have to a gay bar in New West. It's fifties-themed with a jukebox and vinyl booths. Sure enough, Miss Bill knows the owner. He seats us at a table in the window and starts us off with a pair of milkshakes on the house.

"Look at this one," Miss Bill says, as a handsome man walks past the window. "She has biceps, a dog and an attitude."

"Did you really get arrested for doing drag?" I ask him.

"You could get arrested for being gay back in the

day. Men like us stuck out. Doing drag only made it worse."

"I don't know if I'd be willing to go to jail for drag," I say. "Does that make me a bad drag queen?"

"It's different when your life is a crime," Miss Bill says. "The more you hide who you are, the harder you kick down the closet door."

There's a knock on the window. I look and see Ed and Ivan's faces pressed against the glass. Ed points his finger between Miss Bill and I, like he's confused. He takes a picture of us with his phone. Ivan waves hello and my heart melts. I wave back to him and then the two of them walk away without coming in to say hello.

"I recognize your brother," Miss Bill says. "But who is the ginger with the smile and the shoulders?"

"That's Ivan."

"YP — Young and Pretty," Miss Bill says. "My drag mother's intuition tells me something is going on between you two."

"Can you keep a secret?"

"Of course not."

"I don't care, I need to tell someone," I say. "I've been flirting with Ivan behind my brother's back."

"Tell me more!"

"There's not much to tell. I delivered some food to him a few days ago and we've been texting back and forth ever since. I still don't know if he's gay or just a nice guy. I don't want Ed to find out until I know for sure."

"Wouldn't it make more sense to tell your brother so he could ask him if he's gay for you?"

"In a perfect world, yes. But I'm worried if Ed finds out I have a crush on Ivan, he'll tell him I do drag to nip it in the bud. The first guy I ever went on a date with was butch like Ivan and he ghosted me the minute I told him I'm a drag queen."

"Ghosted?"

"Cut off all communication," I explain. "My point is that I'm not ready to be hurt again so soon after my horrible date with Randall."

"Good luck with that," Miss Bill humphs. The waiter puts our bill on the table. Miss Bill takes it out from the sleeve and reviews it. "Ridiculous! Outrageous! I won't pay!" And then he hands the waiter his credit card.

I can't wait to use that line the next time I go out to eat with the Wonder Twins.

07 Fall Ball

THE GYM IS DECORATED with bales of hay and mass-produced plastic pumpkins. The dress code for the annual Fall Ball is Farmer Chic, which translates to overalls and trucker hats for the guys, and short-shorts and plaid tops tied below the breasts for the girls. Kara and I are dressed in our street clothes. Chris is dressed in his usual ensemble of all-black clothing with a straw hat he spray-painted black. High school dances are the closest any of us have come to the gym since grade nine.

"I'd be lying if I said I wasn't mildly turned on by all the cowboys," I say out loud.

"I blame your obsession with Orville Peck," Chris says.

"His voice and masks are just so sexy," I say.

"You're not going to find Orville Peck in this crowd," Kara says.

"I'm going to dance," I say. "You guys coming?"

"You know how I feel about popular music," Chris says.

"'It sounds like it was written in a boardroom,'" Kara and I say in unison.

"Don't be a stick in the mud," Kara says to her brother. "Do you want to look back on your teenage self and see a guy moping by the wall?"

"It's not moping," Chris says. "It's thinking with style."

Kara and I each take one of Chris's hands and drag him onto the dance floor. Chris may pretend he hates dancing to pop music, but he loves it as much as Kara and I do. The three of us can't wait until we're old enough to drink and go clubbing at a real gay bar. In the meantime, we get our groove on at high school dances and throw little parties for ourselves in Kara and Chris's basement.

"Don't look now, but the ghost of dates past is right behind you," Kara shouts into my ear.

I turn around and see Randall dancing behind us. He's wearing a pair of 501s that look cut to the shape of his ass and thighs. I can see his nipples through his T-shirt, the sleeves barely cover his shoulders. He's chewing a piece of straw. He looks like a cowboy in a gay porn. Not that I would know. Randall catches me staring at him. He snarls and turns around. Jerk.

"I need to pee," I shout over the music.

Kara gives me a thumbs-up. Chris is off in his own little world, dancing to the beat of a completely different song than the one that is playing.

It takes my eyes a moment to adjust to the light when I go back into the hall. I'm a little deaf from the loud music. The line for the bathroom goes all the way down to the cafeteria. I'm totally regretting the Red

Bull I had before the dance. Someone punches me hard on the shoulder. It's my brother. Ed's grinning from ear to ear.

"Hey, Joshy," Ed says.

"What did you punch me for?" I say, rubbing my shoulder. "I could have died."

"Dramatic much?" he says. "Look who's here."

Ed steps aside. It's Ivan! And he's talking to Randall. My heart races and sinks at the same time. I want to push Randall out of the way, but I don't want to make a scene. Who am I kidding? I totally want to make a scene.

"Hey, Josh!" Ivan says, like I'm the barista at his local coffee shop instead of the guy who beat him at hockey. "Do you know Randall?"

Randall and I scowl at each other. "Yes, I do," I tell him.

Randall practically yanks Ivan's shoulder to get his attention and says, "What were you saying about *Hamilton?*"

How dare Ivan discuss *Hamilton* with Randall.

That's *our* thing! I grab Ed by the arm and pull him down the hall where it's quieter.

"Why would you bring Ivan to our high school dance?" I ask him.

"I don't know, because he's in high school. And it's something to do on a Friday night," Ed says. "What do you care?"

Crap. If I'm not careful, I could let the cat out of the bag.

"But he doesn't go to our school," I say. I should stop talking. Instead, I say, "He's not even dressed like a cowboy. He probably feels out of place."

"Neither are you."

"I'm not dressed as cowboy out of principle."

"Did someone spike your drink?" Ed says.

"I have to go the bathroom." I leave as quickly as I can before I say anything stupid. I'm so frustrated I can't even pee. I find Kara and Chris on the dance floor where I left them.

"Why the long face?" Kara asks.

"Bitchy rest face," I say.

"Josh is keeping secrets again," Chris says.

"Shut up and dance," I tell him.

I'm not even paying attention to the song I'm dancing to. I keep seeing Randall's beautiful blue eyes beaming as he was talking to Ivan in the hall. I can't compete with that. I'm such a fool for even thinking Ivan was interested in me. He probably only spent time with me because I'm Ed's kid brother.

I look across the dance floor, hoping another face will take my mind off Ivan's. And there's Ivan, dancing just a few people over. He's dancing by himself. Ivan pretends to twerk and then he does the Floss. He's a horrible dancer. It makes me smile. Ivan dances in my direction.

"Did Ed suspect anything?" he asks.

"If he didn't, he does now."

"You ran off so quick. I was worried you went home without saying goodbye."

"Would that have been such a bad thing?"

"Yeah, because I wouldn't have had a chance to ask you out."

My knees go weak.

"You want to go out with me?"

"I thought it was obvious."

"I wasn't sure," I say. "Did Randall say anything about me when you were talking to him?"

"Not at all."

Jerk! I mean, good that Randall didn't say anything. But he's still a jerk.

"So, it's a date?" Ivan says.

"For sure."

"Cool. I'm going to dance by myself again before Ed suspects anything. I'll text you tomorrow."

"I can't wait," I say. I hope I don't sound too thirsty.

"Who was that?" Kara asks after Ivan dances away.

"A friend of Ed's," I say.

"That guy? The one who pretended to twerk?" Kara says. "He doesn't act like one of Ed's friends. He's different."

"I hope so," I say.

08 Nora Desmond

I SHOW UP at Miss Bill's apartment with the high heels we bought at The Bay. I expect to be put through my paces, stomping down the runway in my new shoes until my feet bleed. Instead, we are watching *Sunset Boulevard*, a black-and-white movie about a tired old silent movie actress. Miss Bill's TV is one of the old-fashioned square kind you see in the basement of Value Village with the vacuum cleaners and CD players. He still watches movies on VHS tape. The film is pretty good, but I'm antsy to do drag.

"What does this movie have to do with drag?" I ask.

"Nora Desmond is drag personified!" Miss Bill says. "Look at how she uses her eyes and lips when she speaks. Pay attention to how she moves like a spider, luring her victim into her web."

"It's a little over the top, don't you think?"

"The word you're looking for is 'camp.'"

I start to watch the movie though a drag queen's eyes. I see what Miss Bill is talking about. Nora Desmond is totally lip-syncing for her life. The movie ends. Miss Bill applauds the end credits like he's in a theatre.

"Time to get to work," Miss Bill says, using his cane to get off the couch. "Put those shoes on your feet. I'll be right back."

I stand up in my heels and use the wall for leverage. Miss Bill returns to the living room with a martini in one hand and a vacuum cleaner in the other.

"What's that for?" I ask.

"You don't expect me to do this sober, do you?"

"Not the martini. The vacuum cleaner."

"Darling, this is how I teach all my drag daughters to walk in heels." He puts a classical record on the player and passes the vacuum to me.

"Why do I feel like you're tricking me into vacuuming your apartment?"

"It's one of the advantages of being a drag mother," he says.

I turn on the vacuum and Miss Bill starts speaking to me like a ballet instructor. "Now walk this way."

I follow Miss Bill across the apartment, imitating the way his hips are moving back and forth. He stops and watches as I push the vacuum back across the room.

"Lovely. Now turn around and walk back toward me. Like a lady, Joshua. You're starting to walk like John Wayne in heels."

To my surprise, the vacuum cleaner is helping. I use the handle for support, like a cane. After a couple of passes up and down the living room, I'm starting to get the hang of walking in heels. I've lost all feeling in my toes. The soles of my feet feel like someone is hammering a nail into them. But I feel like a woman.

"That should do for now," Miss Bill says. "I want you to practice that every night. Now tell me about your drag persona."

"I'm serving you Alexander McQueen meets fifties biker chick."

"I understood about two words in that sentence," Miss Bill says. "I don't want to know what you're wearing. I want to know who your drag character is. Is she bitchy? Is she funny? Is she sleazy?"

I've never given my character much thought. I've spent so much time trying to look good for social media, I forgot to develop a character. I have absolutely no idea who I am.

"Do you know who Amy Winehouse is?" I ask Miss Bill.

"I stopped listening to pop music after Madonna," he says. "Why don't you do her for me."

"Now?"

"Do I need to book an appointment?"

"I'm not wearing a dress or make-up."

"A good drag queen doesn't need to be done up to perform. The heels will do."

"Here goes nothing," I say. "Hey, Siri, play 'Back to Black' by Amy Winehouse."

"Who are you talking to?"

"My phone," I say.

The song starts playing. My knees bounce to the opening notes of the piano. My legs feel wobbly from walking in heels. I know this song backward and forward. I sing it in the shower at least once a week. But for whatever reason I can't find myself in the lyrics when I perform them for Miss Bill. The song fades out and I bow my head like the lights have gone out on the stage.

"Beautiful song," Miss Bill says. "She has an amazing voice."

"But what did you think of the performance?"

"I have no idea who she is," he says. "The song is telling me more about the singer than you are."

"It's these damn heels . . ."

"It's not the heels. Lesson number one: When doing drag, be yourself when being someone else. The audience should get a glimpse of the person beneath the make-up. There are a hundred Judy Garland impersonators out there, but there's only one Miss Bill."

"That's not confusing," I say sarcastically.

"Lesson number two: The audience should know who you are trying to portray even if they've never heard of the person. Take this Amy person, for example. What is she famous for?"

"Being a mess."

"That's a perfect entry point for your character."

"But I don't want to demean her. The media mocked her addiction her entire career. I want to celebrate her look and her voice. No singer comes close to Amy Winehouse in my opinion."

"That's exactly how I feel about Judy Garland."

"I can show you a video of one of her songs if you like."

"No. I want you to show me who this woman is

with your drag and your lip-sync. When I can figure out who she is on my own, then my work here is done."

"How am I supposed to be myself and Amy Winehouse at the same time?" I ask.

"Let's start with lyrics of the song. Pull them up on that little pocket computer of yours and we'll go through them line by line."

We spend the rest of the evening sitting at Miss Bill's kitchen table, analyzing the lyrics to "Back to Black." At the end of each line, Miss Bill asks what the lyric means to me and what images come to my head. It's like we're solving a math puzzle. Two hours go by without my even noticing. If this is work, then sign me up.

09 Flat Tire

I GET INTO IVAN'S CAR a couple of blocks away from home. Ivan's face lights up when he sees me. No one knows where I am. I need to stop keeping all these secrets from people. I worry that if our date falls apart the way it did with Randall, my friends and family will think I'm punching too high.

I'm not sure what to do when I get in the car. Should I give Ivan a kiss on the cheek? Ivan seems just as confused as I do. He punches me on the shoulder like I just scored a goal at a hockey game.

"How's it going, bro?" he says.

"Did you just call me 'bro'?"

"Sorry. I play a lot of pick-up hockey with straight guys."

"It's cool, bro," I joke. "What do you want to do, bro?"

"Want to go to a gay bar?" he suggests.

"We're not old enough to drink," I remind him.

"It's early. Maybe they're not checking ID yet."

"My mother warned me about boys like you," I joke. "Sure. Let's go to a gay bar."

Ivan points the car in the direction of the highway. We're starting to see signs for Canada Way when the car starts to bump and thump like it's broken a heel.

"Hey, bro," I say. "I think you have a flat."

"For real?" Ivan says. He pulls over to the side of the road. We both get out to look at the tire. It's flatter than a supermodel from the nineties.

"Do you know how to change a tire?" he asks.

"Yes. Don't you?"

"In theory, yes. But I've never actually done it before."

I'm wearing my favourite jeans and shirt. But now is not the time to be a princess. "I'll change the tire," I say. "But I get to pick the bar."

"It's so cool you can change a tire," Ivan says.

"It's a good thing you're pretty," I tell him as I assemble the jack.

The lights of Vancouver get brighter as we cross the Georgia Viaduct into the city. I love driving into Vancouver. It makes my heart race every time. I plan to live here one day. Or anywhere that has a large gay population where I can make a living doing drag.

"So where are we going?" Ivan asks.

"Have you ever heard of a place called Poodles?" I ask him.

"Sounds like a dog groomer," he says.

"It's a drag bar," I say, wincing a little.

"I don't know how I feel about going to a drag bar," he says.

"You don't like drag?"

"I don't get it," he says. "Where is the talent in dressing up as a woman and pretending to sing a song?"

Looks like I won't be telling him I do drag on our first date.

"I doubt there's a drag show on now," I say. "It's not even seven."

"We made a deal," Ivan says, smiling. "And I always honour my agreements."

Ivan finds a parking spot a few feet away from Poodles.

"OMG! Doris Day parking," I squeal. Did that sound as gay I think it did? I lower my voice, undo my seatbelt and say, "Well, here goes nothing."

We walk up to the bar entrance. Ivan was right. The doorman isn't working yet. Ivan holds the door open for me and we walk right in. I've only ever been to Poodles during the day for Drag Brunch with Kara and Chris. After sundown, the dance floor is open and the place turns into a full-on bar. Tonight is Drag Bingo.

"Why does that drag queen have a beard and moustache?" Ivan asks.

"That's tough drag," I tell him. "It pokes fun at drag."

I notice that all eyes are on our table. At first, I think they've clocked us as underage teens. Then I realize they're all staring at Ivan. He is by far the most attractive guy in the room. A waiter appears out of nowhere, carrying a tray. He looks into Ivan's eyes and asks in a sexy voice, "Can I get you anything?"

"I'll have a Coke, please," Ivan says.

"Are you sure you just want a Coke?" the waiter purrs. "There's so much more I can offer you."

"A Coke will do," Ivan says, a little uncomfortably.

The waiter snarls like a tiger. He's about to walk off without taking my order.

"I'd like a drink too!" I say, reminding him that I exist. "Can I have a cranberry . . . vodka."

Ivan looks at me like I've blown our cover. The

waiter gives me the once over. If I wasn't here with Ivan, he would totally ID me. But I *am* with Ivan, and if I leave, so does he. The waiter walks off and returns with our drinks. I'm almost positive there's no vodka in mine, but I'm not going to tell Ivan that.

The Bingo portion of the evening ends and the DJ takes over the festivities from the drag host. The first song is "Dance to This" by Troye Sivan and Ariana Grande.

"Want to dance?" I ask Ivan.

"You've seen me dance," he says. "I'm awful."

"All you have to do is hold me in your arms and sway your hips," I tell him.

Ivan thinks about it and says, "I think I can manage that."

We walk out onto the dance floor. I wrap my arms around Ivan's neck and look into his eyes as we sway to the music. Everyone is watching us, eating their hearts out. I am *loving* this.

"You looked really sexy when you were changing that tire earlier," Ivan says.

"Really?"

"Really."

"Cool," I say, imitating him.

No one has ever told me I'm sexy. And just when I think the night can't get any better, Ivan leans his face into mine and kisses me softly on the lips. I think I can chalk up this date as a success.

10 Halloween

EVERY HALLOWEEN, the Wonder Twins and I get together in their basement and watch old horror movies. They have to be old because the newer horror movies are too scary for Kara and me. Horror movies are basically rom-coms for Chris. This year we're watching *Whatever Happened to Baby Jane*, on Miss Bill's recommendation.

I'm applying black and orange nail polish in honour of the holiday. My phone rings. The only people who ever call me are Mom and Kara, and only when it's an emergency. Since Mom is watching TV, I assume Kara wants me to pick something up last-minute on the way to her place. I absentmindedly swipe my phone, too focused on my nails to look at the caller ID.

"Hey, Josh!" a friendly voice says on the phone.

"Ivan?" I say. I take Ivan off speaker so Ed won't hear. "I thought you were going to a party with your hockey bros tonight."

"I thought it would be more fun to spend Halloween with you."

That's so sweet. But what am I going to do? I can't show up at Kara and Chris's with Ivan on my arm. They both have an aversion to anyone who can lift heavy things.

"I have plans to see scary movies at a friend's house," I say.

"Cool," he says, sounding disappointed.

"Want to come?" I ask sheepishly.

"Sure, if your friends won't mind."

"They won't mind," I lie.

I give Ivan the address. I grab the treats I bought and then race to Kara and Chris's as fast as I can on my bike. Their grandmother, who doesn't speak a word of English, answers the door. Grandma owns the house the Wonder Twins live in. She's a devout Christian. I'm positive Grandma blames me for Kara and Chris being queer. Every time I come over she pretends not to know me. Kara finally comes to the door to let me into the house.

"I have to tell you something," I say, still out of breath from the bike ride over.

"Who's that?" Kara says, as Ivan's car pulls up into the driveway.

"Surprise! I have a boyfriend," I tell her. "And he doesn't know I do drag."

"Hey, Josh," Ivan says, getting out of the car with a bag of snacks in his hand. Grandma's face lights up as Ivan comes up the front steps of the house. Of course she likes *him*. She probably thinks he's there to see Kara. Ivan gives me a peck on the cheek and the look of excitement on Grandma's face fades. She goes back into the house, looking disappointed.

"Ivan this is Kara, Kara this is Ivan," I say as fast as I can. "Why don't you two get the snacks together and get to know each other while I go downstairs and say hi to Chris."

I don't give them a chance to respond. Instead, I fly down the stairs to the basement like the Road Runner. Chris is sprawled in an old recliner, watching a slasher movie. He startles when he sees me.

"No time to explain," I say. "I brought a date and he doesn't know about Siri Alexa."

"Am I having a nightmare?" Chris asks.

"We'll find out soon enough," I say.

Kara and Ivan come down the stairs carrying bowls of chips, popcorn and candy. Ivan places the snacks on an old coffee table and offers his hand to Chris to shake, like he's at a job interview. Which he kind of is.

"I'm Ivan. You must be Chris."

"Are those full-sized chocolate bars?" Chris says,

pointing to the candy bowl on the coffee table.

"I brought those," Ivan says. "I hope you like Snickers."

"He can stay for now," Chris says to me, taking a chocolate bar.

Ivan and I take a seat on the couch together. He takes my hand in his and says, "Are you wearing nail polish?"

The Wonder Twins look surprised, like the cat is already out of the bag.

"It's my costume," I say. "I came as candy corn."

"Cool," says Ivan.

Kara and Chris roll their eyes at how gullible Ivan is.

The movie is like nothing I've ever seen before. It's like a horror movie with drag queens that are being played by cisgender women. Me, Kara and Chris laugh all through the movie. The movie is exactly our jam. Ivan looks confused, uncomfortable even. He seems relieved when it's over.

"That was the best movie in the world," Chris says.

"It was kind of long," Ivan says. "What made you want to see *that* movie?"

"Miss Bill recommended it to Josh," Kara says.

"*Miss* Bill?" Ivan asks.

"Josh, don't be a drag," Chris teases. "Tell Ivan who Miss Bill is."

"They're talking about my downstairs neighbour," I explain.

"The old man who dresses like a woman in daylight?" says Ivan. "Ed said you hated that guy when we saw you at the Unicorn together. That's why he took a picture."

"Bill and I have come to an understanding," I say. "I help him out around the apartment."

"Help him out how?" Ivan asks.

"Chris, can you hand me the popcorn?" Kara asks. "This is getting good."

"I buy him his Depends diapers," I say off the top of my head.

"And you kiss your *mother* with that mouth?" Chris says.

I glare at Chris. There's only one way out of this.

"Ivan and I went to a gay bar," I say.

"You went to a gay bar without us?" Kara says, spilling the popcorn bowl onto the floor.

"We made a pact that we would all go to our first gay bar together," Chris says.

"Oh, well," I say. I pretend to look at an invisible watch on my wrist. "Would you look at the time."

I can't get Ivan out of there fast enough. We load my bike into the trunk of his car.

"I don't think your friends like me," he says.

"Don't worry about those two," I tell him. "They're like parents. In their eyes, no one is good enough for me."

11 Family Resemblance

I'M TRYING TO SIT STILL while Miss Bill paints my face. He insists the queens of my generation have taken contouring too far and wants me to try a more natural look. I'm not used to someone putting their hands this close to my eyes and mouth unless they're a healthcare professional.

"Can I look now?" I ask.

"For the hundredth time, no. And if you don't sit still, I'm going to paint your face so you look like Divine."

"Who's that?"

"Add her to the list of people to Boggle."

"Google."

"Whatever. You kids are always so busy looking at your gadgets you can't see what's in front of you." Miss Bill takes a step back to admire his work. "How are things with the ginger?"

"Amazing! We text every day and we've gone out five times. Once to an escape room where we didn't even try to escape and just made out. And we went swimming at the Canada Games Pool where I got to see him naked in the change room, so that was cool."

"How romantic."

"I know, right? And just the other day, Ivan came out to my brother."

"So, your brother knows you're dating his friend?"

"God, no! The last thing I need is Ed telling Ivan I do drag."

"What's to prevent him from doing that now?"

"If Ed knows that I'm dating Ivan, he'll tell him I do drag to embarrass me. But as long as Ed thinks

Ivan and I have nothing to do with each other, he won't mention it because *he'll* be embarrassed. If I can keep our relationship a secret a little while longer, that should give me time to tell Ivan myself."

"You're operating on very slim margins, don't you think?" Miss Bill says. "I recommend coming clean the first chance you get."

"Have you ever hidden your drag from a boyfriend?"

"Of course! Granted, things were different when I was a pretty young thing and had more gentleman callers than cash. It was hard enough telling another man you were attracted to him, much less a drag queen. Back then the only drag queen on TV was Milton Berle."

"Who's Milton . . ."

"Google it!"

"It must have been easier after Stonewall."

Miss Bill raises his hands to the ceiling. "Praise the Goddess, he knows what Stonewall is."

"I wasn't raised under a rock."

"I've had my doubts," Miss Bill says. "The answer is no. In the seventies and eighties, everyone was trying to look like a cop or construction worker. The only thing drag queens were good for was raising money. So, yes, I was known to keep my drag a secret from a man. Especially if I wanted to have sex with him. It made things easier."

"Then I don't feel so bad about not telling Ivan."

"Are you waiting until he proposes?"

"He's a jock! His idea of fashion is shower sandals and gym socks. There aren't a lot of gay guys my age in this neck of the woods. I can't let this one slip through my fingers."

"I can't say I blame you. Some men have such a narrow view of what it means to be a man. They can't wrap their heads around the idea that masculinity comes in all shapes and forms. Dressing up as a woman doesn't mean you're not masculine. Take me, for example. You would never confuse me for a real woman when I'm in drag."

"I never thought about masculinity that way

before," I say. "I wish I could go back in time to my date with Randall and get in his face about his masculine-acting BS."

"It is so strange to discuss gay dating with someone who is still in high school," Miss Bill says. His face is concentrating on mine. "What is it like being a gay teenager in this day and age?"

"It's not bad," I say. "They still make fun of us."

"Oh, darling, they will always make fun of us."

"I can't imagine what it would be like to hide my sexuality. It's hard enough keeping my drag a secret from Ivan."

"That's why I became a drag queen," Miss Bill says. "I got so sick of pretending to be something I wasn't, I took it to the opposite extreme."

"It would be harder if I didn't have Kara and Chris to lean on. I'm worried they're feeling neglected because of Ivan."

"Things always change with your friends when you start a relationship. They'll be fine. It's good that you have friends your age to discuss what you're going through. I didn't have that until my twenties."

"You never talk about your friends."

"They're all dead," Miss Bill says matter-of-factly. He points to the poster of the Great Pretenders. "AIDS got them all. We raised so much money trying to find a cure. But the pills came too late for them."

I've heard bits and pieces about the AIDS crisis in the eighties. But this is the first time I've been able to put a face to the disease. Miss Bill stops what he's doing for a moment, like he's forgotten where he is. Then he shakes it off and holds a mirror up to my face.

"Voila! What do you think?"

I look like my mother her in graduation photo.

"I love it!" I say.

12 Code Blue

I'VE GOT MY HEADPHONES ON while I vacuum the apartment in my heels. I'm working on the lyrics of "You Know I'm No Good" by Amy Winehouse. My goal is to be able to perform all the songs on the *Back to Black* album by Christmas.

Mom comes home from work looking exhausted. She's looked haggard ever since she found out Dad was fooling around with Becky. Mom is standing there, frozen in the living room, holding a bag of groceries.

"Are those my heels?" she asks.

"I bought them at The Bay."

"I'm not sure what the right answer to that question was," she says. "Careful with those things. You'll hurt yourself."

I turn the vacuum cleaner off and hear more keys in the door.

"Is anyone home?" Ed shouts.

"Me and Mom are," I shout back.

"Ivan is with me!"

I have two seconds to get rid of my heels before Ed and Ivan come into the living room. I see the open closet where we keep the vacuum cleaner and launch each heel into it like I'm making a field goal. I rush to close the closet door just as Ed and Ivan come into the room, their cheeks still red from playing a pick-up game of hockey.

"Hey, Ivan," I say. "Long time no see."

"Yes," Ivan says. "I don't believe we've seen each other since the high school dance."

"I believe you are correct," I say.

Ed looks at us awkwardly.

"I'm not sure what that was about," Ed says. "Let me drop off my equipment and change before we head out."

I wait for Ed to leave the room and whisper to Ivan, "What are you doing here? Why didn't you text to give me a heads up?"

"I haven't had time!" Ivan whispers back. "I need to tell you something quick. Ed told his friend Randall that I'm gay. Now Randall wants to go out on a date with me."

"What did you say?"

"I didn't say anything. I wanted to tell you first."

"Do you *want* to go on a date with Randall?"

"I barely know the guy. We talked for all of ten minutes at the dance."

"He's good-looking though," I say.

"He's very good-looking," Ivan says.

"What's that supposed to mean?"

"I was agreeing with you!" Ivan says. "Ed is going to come out of that room any minute now. What do you want me to do?"

"This is a lot of pressure to put on me out of the blue," I say. "Do I have to give you an answer right now?"

"Think about it and text me later," Ivan says.

Ed walks into the living room and sees us chatting intensely.

"Everything all right?" he asks.

"I still can't get over what an amazing job Josh did on this couch," Ivan says. He follows Ed toward the door, then stops to mouth, "Text me."

I sit there for a minute, not believing what I just heard. Of course, I don't want Ivan going on a date with Randall. They're perfect for each other. If Randall takes his shirt off in front of Ivan, it's game over between us.

"I'm stepping out, Mom," I shout toward the kitchen.

"Where are you going?" she asks. "I was just about to start dinner."

"I'm just going to check in on Bill downstairs really quick."

"You hate that guy!"

"We kissed and made up. TTFN."

I run downstairs to Miss Bill's apartment. He answers the door wearing a silk robe and his face is covered in cream.

"Code blue, code blue," I say, pushing past him into the apartment.

"Is someone having a heart attack? Should I call 911?"

"Worse. My brother set up my rival, Randall, on a date with Ivan."

"Did Ivan accept?"

"He wants me to decide for him."

"Then tell him no!"

"What if Ivan resents me for telling him not to go on the date? Wouldn't it be better if let him go on the date? That way he can find out for himself that Randall is a jerk."

"Why not tell your brother you're dating his friend?"

"And risk Ed spilling the beans about my drag ambitions?"

"Didn't you tell your so-called rival you do drag? He could tell Ivan as easily as your brother."

"I follow Randall on Twitter. He only ever talks about himself."

"What's a Twitter?" Miss Bill asks. "Never mind, I don't care. You could put an end to all this if you told Ivan you do drag."

"But that could end my relationship with Ivan faster than Randall," I say. "At the same time, without drag, I'm running out of ways to keep in him interested in me unless I want to tell him about my homework."

"You're being too hard on yourself," Miss Bill says. "You're a lovely boy. In the brief time we've spent with each other, I can tell that you're very creative and talented. I'm sure that's what Ivan is attracted to."

"What if I do tell Ivan not to go out with Randall? Won't he just wonder what he's missing out on?"

"There's always going to be someone better out there, even if it's only for a couple of hours," Miss Bill says.

"You're no comfort whatsoever."

"You could always let Ivan go on the date and then follow him in drag."

"That idea is so ridiculous it might actually work."

"What's a drag mother for if not ridiculous ideas made while getting drunk on dirty martinis?"

I give Miss Bill a peck on the forehead and get face cream all over my lips. I go back upstairs and text Ivan that he should go on the date with Randall. Then I text the Wonder Twins and ask them if they want to go on an adventure.

13 Spy Kids

IVAN DIDN'T SEEM the least bit suspicious when I asked where Randall was taking him on their date. It makes me wonder if I should have more faith in him. He's probably going on the date to be nice, like he said he was. At the same time, I can't take that chance. I need to see with my own eyes how he gets on with Randall.

I get into drag at Kara and Chris's house. Kara is also going in drag to avoid arousing suspicion.

Grandma shakes her head when she sees the both of us in Kara's room switching genders.

"How do we look?" I ask Chris.

"Like you need better lighting," he says.

"You're not going like that, are you?" Kara says. "They'll recognize you."

"Randall doesn't see me when I walk past him in the halls at school," Chris says. "He definitely won't notice me at a restaurant."

"Put my clothes on," I say. "No one will recognize you in primary colours."

We drive to the Dugout in their parents' car. It's a crisp November Saturday afternoon. I thank the Goddess it isn't raining, or it would ruin the three layers of wigs I used to create my Amy Winehouse hair. I check myself one last time in the rearview mirror before we get out of the car.

"You look good," Kara says. "Miss Bill would be proud."

"Kara's right," Chris says. "Your drag suits you now."

"Thanks, I needed to hear that," I say. "Now let's keep Randall's claws off my boyfriend."

We spot Ivan and Randall right away. They're seated at a table near the window where everyone on the street can see them. I lower my head so they won't recognize me.

"Chin up, face forward and flashy those pearly whites of yours," Kara says.

I throw my shoulders back and walk into the Dugout like the diva I am.

"Table for three please," I say to the first person I see.

"I don't work here," the person says.

"Rude," Chris mutters.

We are seated far enough away from Randall and Ivan's table that they can't see us. A pair of swishy queens wearing checkered curling pants comes to our table to pay their respects to Kara and me. One of them tells me Abundance O'Caution, the manager at Poodles, is looking at new acts for her show.

"She is?" I say, taking my eyes off Ivan and Randall

for a second.

"She can be a harsh bitch, so make sure you know all your words or she will read you to filth," says one of the curlers.

"She knows from experience," says the other, gesturing at her friend.

The curling queens finally leave our table. I go right back to staring at Ivan and Randall. They look like they're having a good time. Too good a time. They look like they were made for each other. Both of them are handsome and athletic. I look like Ed's little sister by comparison.

"Are you okay?" Kara asks. "We can go."

"Not yet," I say. "I need a sign that Ivan is into him. Once I have that, I can have some closure on this whole experience."

Ivan gets up from the table. He's looking around the restaurant for something. His eyes meet mine and he starts walking toward our table. My heart swells in anticipation. He slows down like he recognizes me. Then he continues to walk past us with confidence and follows the sign pointing toward the restrooms.

"It's time to go," I say.

"We haven't paid the bill," says Chris.

"I don't want to be here when he kisses Randall," I say. "I might drive my heel into Randall's head."

"I'll get the bill," Kara says. "You guys go wait for me in the car."

I avoid making eye contact with anyone on the sidewalk as I walk back to the car. I don't want them seeing the eyeliner running down my face. What's strange is that this is the closest I've felt to Amy Winehouse since I started doing her in drag. This is how she must have felt when her husband was in jail. As heartbroken as I am, I force myself to remember this moment for when I'm performing "Back to Black."

Mom doesn't even bat an eye when I come home dressed as woman. I de-drag and then go downstairs to see Miss Bill. He's wearing a peach pantsuit and a pair of fuzzy slippers.

"You look like Bette Davis unearthed," he says when he sees me.

"If that's supposed to mean I look terrible, it's because I feel terrible," I say.

Miss Bill invites me in. I fall dramatically on the couch. The fake fireplace is on. An old movie is playing on the TV. Miss Bill pours me a cup of tea. His apartment is cozy, like the velvety insides of a jewelry box.

"I take it your spy mission did not go well," Miss Bill says.

"He looked me right in the eye and didn't recognize me."

"That was the point of going in disguise," Miss Bill reminds me.

"Shouldn't he have sensed it was me?" I ask. "I thought we had a deeper connection than that."

"You're being dramatic, even for a drag queen," Miss Bill says. There's a knock on the door. "I wonder who that could be."

Miss Bill gets up from his lounge chair and presses his face against the peephole. He opens the door and the light from the hall casts a shadow on the visitor.

"Is Josh here?" Ivan says, entering the apartment. He looks around like he's stepped into a haunted house. He smiles when he sees me.

"I'll go make myself a martini," Miss Bill says.

I sit up on the couch to make space for Ivan. He sits next to me, still distracted by Miss Bill's apartment.

"How was your date with Randall?" I ask.

"He wanted to know how much I bench press," Ivan says. "I think it's time we told Ed we're dating. I never want to have to go on a date like that again."

I take Ivan into my arms and hug him until he can't breathe. Then I pepper his face with kisses. Ivan looks stunned when I finally stop.

"Let me tell Ed," I say. "It will be better coming from me."

And I can ask Ed not to tell Ivan I do drag until I'm ready.

14 Strange Bromance

IVAN AND I ARE GLIDING around the ice rink at Robson Square. I forgot how much I love ice skating. It's so easy to get lost in the moment as the world whips past you. I like the sound of my blades against the ice and the sound of children laughing as their parents pull them along the rink.

"You're a good skater, Josh," Ivan says.

"When I told my dad I didn't want to play hockey anymore, I asked him if I could try figure skating," I tell him. "He said it was too expensive. But I think it was too gay for him."

"I love figure skating," Ivan says. "It requires so much strength and concentration."

"And those asses and thighs are nothing to sneeze at."

"I never noticed," Ivan says, giving me a friendly nudge.

"I think you like figure skating because of the sparkly outfits," I tease.

"That's not true," Ivan says.

"Admit it. Figure skating brings out your feminine side."

"I like figure skating for its artistry."

"Liar," I say mischievously.

"Stop it, Joshua!" Ivan says.

He sounds like my father when I act too gay around him. I'm taken aback by how irritated he is. I let go of Ivan's hand to give him his space. I'm trying not to act like a princess. The fact that I'm censoring my emotions so I'm not 'acting like a girl' only reinforces our differences. It was a joke. If I can't tease Ivan about being feminine, how is he going to respond when I tell him I do drag?

Ivan shakes it off. He holds out his hand for me to take. I consider it for a moment. Then I reach out. Someone skates between us just as our fingers are about to touch. We are swarmed by three guys in hockey jerseys. My heart races. Are we being bashed? I notice our attackers crawling all over Ivan like they just won a hockey game. I calm down a little. They're pretty aggressive, though.

"How are you, my man?" the biggest of the three says.

"Why didn't you tell us you were coming skating? You could have joined us," says another.

This should be interesting.

"Hey, guys, have you met Ed's brother Joshua?" Ivan says. "Josh, this is Jason, Ted and Mike from the Dream Factory."

"Hey, buddy," Mike says.

I wave meekly. If there was a lake nearby, I would go jump in it.

"Is Ed here?" Jason asks.

This is awkward. I watch as Ivan looks for the right answer. I drive the tip of my blade in the ice and stop on the spot. I cross my arms in front of my sweater and give Ivan the what-for with my glare.

"We're on a date," Ivan says, like he was possessed by a demon.

"Whoa!" the three of them say in unison. They start to shove Ivan and mess up his hair like he's a stud and I'm a bikini-clad babe in a beer ad. Ivan starts blushing at the attention.

Any normal person would have wished us a good night when they learned we were on a date. Not these guys. They can't comprehend that we're a couple. Instead, they continue skating with us.

"Get a load of the tits on that chick!" says Ted. "I would love to motorboat those."

"Ted's balls are bluer than a Smurf's," Jason says.

"Show us your blue balls, buddy," says Mike. He grabs the waistband of Ted's sweatpants and pulls them down around his ankles. Ted falls, nearly taking a kid with him. Mike and Jason dogpile onto Ted and they start playfighting on the ice. They look like idiots. If this is what masculinity is, they can have it. Just when I think that I can't get any more annoyed, I see Ivan laughing at their antics. I skate off toward the benches to put my shoes on.

"What's going on?" Ivan asks when he catches up to me.

"You tell me," I say. "One minute we're holding hands and having a nice time, the next minute I'm at the Royal Rumble."

"They were just horsing around," he says.

"That might be horsing around to you because you can pass for straight," I say. "But for guys like me that can't, that's foreplay for a gay-bashing."

"Aren't you being a little dramatic?"

"You think this is dramatic?" I say, trying not to cock my head. "You don't know what dramatic is."

People are looking. This is going to end up on YouTube if I don't tone it down. Randall would love that. I tie my shoes aggressively, wanting to get out of there as fast as I can. Ivan kicks off his skates and starts following me in his stocking feet.

"I work with those guys," Ivan says. "What did you expect me to do? Tell them to act their age?"

"That's exactly what I expected you to do!"

"I get that your circle of friends is gay. But mine isn't! It was a big deal for me to come out to those guys. I don't want to make them uncomfortable around me because I'm gay."

"You had no problem making me uncomfortable when I accused you of getting in touch with your feminine side."

"That's because *you* were making *me* uncomfortable!"

"Then it's a good thing you haven't put your shoes on," I say. "You still have time to lace up your skates and all be comfortable together!"

I storm off into the night, feeling empowered and depressed at the same time. I think I may have just ended my first relationship ever.

15 Cat Fight

I HAVEN'T SPOKEN to Ivan in two days. I want to call him, but I feel he should be the one to call first. I'm worried that he's *really* mad at me. What if I made him so angry, he doesn't want to have anything to do with me? Have we broken up? I don't even know. I've never had a boyfriend before, much less had an argument with one. As much as I want to see Ivan, I get angry all over again whenever I replay our date in my mind.

All of this is going through my head as I prepare to present my Amy Winehouse drag to Miss Bill in his living room. It's taken a couple of weeks and a whole lot of food delivery app runs to nail down her signature look. My neck hurts from keeping the three wigs on top of my head. I'm serving Egyptian eyeliner and a vintage mechanic's shirt with rolled up sleeves, tied in the front to show off my black bra. My handmade sixties-inspired mini-skirt comes halfway down my thighs. I used eyelash glue and a silver bead for the piercing above her lip. My knees are slightly bent toward each other the way hers were when she was on stage. She always looked so vulnerable, despite the power of her voice.

"How do I look?" I ask Miss Bill.

"The higher the hair, the closer to God," he says.

"What's that supposed to mean?" I ask defensively.

"It's a saying from the sixties," he says. "I love what you've done with your wigs. The shirt has a Rosie the Riveter quality that I adore. This is good. This is *really* good. It opens you up to songs from the fifties and sixties."

"Do you get who she is, though?"

"I think so. You look like one of the Ronettes. Pretty and tough, like you would punch a guy if he messed with you."

"But vulnerable."

"Show me her vulnerability through song, then," he says. I wait for Miss Bill to make himself comfortable. He curls his feet under his silk robe, which spreads around him on the lounge chair like a dress. He takes a sip from his martini and says, "Whenever you're ready."

"Hey, Siri," I shout to my iPhone. "Play 'Rehab' by Amy Winehouse."

My first mistake was choosing a song without an intro. Amy leaps into the first verse like she's desperate for a drink, which she probably was when she recorded the song. I try to imitate her jittery dance moves she used on stage in the years before she died. I slice the air with my hand when she says, "No, no, no," just like she did in the music video. I try to capture how she stumbled around the stage as if she didn't know where she was. I focus on the words, tilt my shoulders back and forth seductively. Whatever I'm doing, it's not working. I can see it in Miss Bill's face. It's easy to tell when you're bombing, even if it's for an audience of one. I curtsey when the song ends, and nearly fall over in my heels.

Miss Bill claps limply.

"I take it she had a substance abuse problem," Miss Bill says.

"Booze and heroin."

"You're overdoing it. It looks like you're making fun of her. I need to feel empathy for her."

"Did you not see how I totally changed my posture?"

"It's a song about addiction and you performed it like someone deciding what to wear to the prom."

"If you had any idea what I've been going through with Ivan you wouldn't be so hard on me. It took all I had to pull this number together."

"I've experienced more heartache than you will ever know in your lifetime and I still managed to bring the house down."

"Spare me the lecture. This isn't about me and my performance. This is about you and your faded glory. You're jealous because my star is rising and yours is setting into the horizon."

Miss Bill's face is as red as his silk robe. He gets up from the lounge chair and bumps into me with his shoulder as he walks to the record player. I get a glimpse of the tough-as-nails drag queen that performed at logging camps in the seventies. He pulls an album from his collection, his fingers knowing its exact location. *Judy, Judy, Judy* is written vertically down the front of the orange album cover.

"Sit," he says.

I do as I'm told. Miss Bill puts the needle on the record. Bongos start playing. Miss Bill stiffens like he's been struck by lightning. He snaps his head toward me like he's possessed. His fingers flutter electrically. His eyes are open as wide as they will go. Miss Bill dives into the song like it's a pool on a hot summer's day. He's all over his living the room, performing to the adoring audience on the album. He climbs onto the furniture and rolls on the floor like he's a maniac. He's not wearing an ounce of make-up, a wig or a dress. Yet now I know exactly who Judy Garland was and why so many gay men loved her.

When the song is done, Miss Bill gets up off the floor and dusts off his silk robe. He grabs his cane, wincing in pain.

"That is the level of performance I expect from my drag daughters," he says. "Nothing less. If you can't handle the heat, I suggest you get out of the kitchen, missy."

"I'm sorry. I didn't mean what I said."

"Get out," Miss Bill says.

"I said I was sorry!"

Miss Bill walks over to the door and opens it for me. I stand my ground, refusing to leave.

"I can stand here all day," Miss Bill says.

I give up and walk out the door.

16 Amy's Ghost

I CONVINCE MOM that I'm coming down with the flu and that I need to stay home from school. Mom puts up a bit of a fuss and then relents. Ed sees right through me.

"Faker," he says, as he leaves to go to school.

I stay in bed until I'm sure the apartment is empty. I would hide under the covers until graduation if I could. The only thing that gets me back on my feet is the bathroom. I look at my reflection in the mirror as I wash my hands. I can still see the outline of Amy Winehouse painted onto my face.

"Hey, Siri," I say in Amy's British accent. "Play 'Back to Black' by Amy Winehouse."

The song starts to play. I'm teleported from my room to a basement jazz bar. I'm standing on a small stage, a quartet squeezed in behind me. The dim light from the stage casts shadows across the faces of people sitting at small round tables. Cigarette smoke rises from ashtrays. I perform the song's soulful lyrics for the audience like they're a long-lost love. I feel every note in my bones. I've never felt so sad in all my life and it all comes out through the song. I draw my hand down in front of my face like I'm pulling down a curtain and bow to the audience in my imagination. When I stand up again, I'm back in our bathroom.

Did I just dream that? Or did I really perform the song as good as it looked in the mirror?

I quickly get back into my Amy Winehouse drag. I carry my heels in my hands as I go down the stairs so I that I don't trip and fall. I bang on Miss Bill's door.

He doesn't answer so I bang some more. Miss Bill comes to the door, his robe pulled up close to his throat. So, this is what he looks like without make-up on.

"I'm not speaking to you," he says.

"If you let me in, I promise I will make it up to you for last night."

"This better be good," Miss Bill huffs, and pushes the door open for me. "I'm missing *Days of our Lives* for this."

I return to my spot in the living room and wait for Miss Bill to take his seat on the lounge chair.

"Hey, Siri! Play 'Back to Black' by Amy Winehouse," I tell my phone.

"I'll never get used to that," Miss Bill says.

The song begins to play and I transform into Amy Winehouse once again. Her movements come to me naturally now, her words are my words, her eyes are my eyes. I teleport back to the jazz bar in my mind. Except this time, Miss Bill is sitting at one of the round tables, staring up at me smiling. The song echoes away and I bow my head.

"That was everything I've been trying to teach you to do," Miss Bill says. "What changed?"

"A broken heart," I say.

"If I had known that, I would have hired an escort for Ivan ages ago," Miss Bill says. "You never did tell me what happened between you two."

"He was being the 'Hockey Type,'" I say with air quotes.

"Translation, please," he says.

"Straight-acting."

"Ah, I see. Have you two talked about it yet?"

"Nope. I'm still waiting for him to call."

"Don't wait too long. You don't want to 'ghost' yourself out of a relationship."

"Have you ever seen a side of someone that made you question your feelings for them?"

"How much time do you have?"

"I'm being serious."

"So am I. No one guy is going to tick off all the boxes of your perfect boyfriend checklist," Miss Bill says. "Managing your differences is what relationships are all about."

"That's if Ivan and I are still in a relationship."

"Enough about boys. How did you feel up there?"

"Amazing! It was like she was speaking directly through me."

"We need to get you on stage. I'm taking you to Poodles on Saturday afternoon to introduce you to Abundance O'Caution."

"That's in two days! I'm not ready."

"Yes, you are. Do the other number, the one about rehab. What's it called again?"

"'Rehab,'" I say.

"If you're going to repeat everything I say, then we're not going to get anywhere," Miss Bill says. "I don't care what it's called. You go back upstairs and start working on that number."

I go home feeling slightly better than when I left. I check my phone to see if I missed a call or text. All I see on my home screen is the time. I put the phone to my lips, preparing to ask Siri to call Ivan for me. But I put the phone away. I want to end the day on a high note.

17 Poodles

MISS BILL AND I are inching up Davie Street in the pink Cadillac, causing a traffic jam. Car horns are blaring behind us. I sink below the dashboard, embarrassed.

"You're not going to find Doris Day parking on Davie Street on a Saturday afternoon," I say.

"I'm going to drop you off at Poodles. Go make nice with Abundance O'Caution while I find parking."

"The whole point of you coming with me was to introduce me to Abundance."

"Fly, little bird, fly," Miss Bill says, pulling over to let me out of the car. "You'll do fine until I get there."

I'm greeted with whistles and cheers as I get out of the car. I feel like a celebrity getting out of a limo at the Oscars. I wait until there is absolutely no traffic coming in either direction before crossing the street. My phone starts buzzing when I get to the other side. I look at my phone. Ivan's face appears on the home screen, smiling back at me. I decline the call, even though I'm dying to speak to him. Now is not the time.

Poodles is decorated for Christmas. The restaurant is mostly empty. I clomp over to the bar and climb up onto one of the barstools. A large woman in a gold dress and huge blonde hair has her back to me behind the bar.

"Excuse me," I say.

When she turns around, I see that she has a big, bushy handlebar moustache. It's the drag queen from Bingo.

"Can I get you something?" she grunts.

"I'm not here for a drink," I say.

"That's music to a bartender's ears."

"I'm looking for Abundance O'Caution."

"You found her," she says. "Let me guess. You want to audition for a spot in my show."

"How did you know?"

"The wig was a dead giveaway. And I recognize you from Instagram. If you think beating your face within an inch of its life is the same thing as putting on a show, it's not."

"I know that!" I say. "I've been practicing my act for over a month now. I'm good. I promise."

"Is this man bothering you, Siri?" Miss Bill says from the doorway of Poodles.

"Miss Bill!" Abundance says, like she's seen a ghost.

"I feel like Norma Desmond returning to the Paramount lot," Miss Bill says as he takes a seat at the bar. "Pour your drag mother a dirty martini, darling."

"I don't work here," I say.

"The one with the moustache," Miss Bill says.

"*She's* your drag mother?" Abundance asks me, pouring vodka and olive juice into a martini glass. "Did she make you vacuum her apartment in heels?"

"Yes, and she has the blisters to prove it," Miss Bill says, taking a sip from his drink.

"So, what brings you out of your coffin in daylight?" Abundance asks.

"I would like you to meet Miss Siri Alexa," Miss Bill says. "I want you to let her audition for you."

"I'm not running a charity, Mother."

"You won't be disappointed," Miss Bill says, raising his eyebrows as he takes another sip from his martini.

Abundance eyes me from head to toe. She looks skeptical and trapped at the same time.

"Here's how it works. If you can get a tip out of one of these cheap queens," Abundance gestures around the bar, "I'll consider putting you on at the beginning of a show. What number are you going to do?"

"'Rehab' by Amy Winehouse," I say.

"Go big or go home, eh?" Abundance says. She shouts to the patrons still in the cafe. "Okay, you bitches . . . Siri Alexa here is going to put on a show for you to sharpen your claws with."

I clomp onto the stage. I look out across the cafe. Ten faces are looking up at me. I should be nervous, and yet I feel like I'm at home. I close my eyes and let Amy enter my body.

"Hit it," I say pointing at the bar.

I dive right into the song. I shimmy across the stage and then go out into the audience. I lie across the tables and sit on laps. Then it happens. I get a five-dollar tip. I nearly break character, I'm so excited. I'm only halfway through the song and I can already feel my life starting over. I get another five-dollar bill and then another! I get a healthy round of applause when I take my bow, then I saunter back to the bar and wave the money in Abundance's face.

"I'm gooped," Abundance says. "How old are you, darling?"

"Sixteen," I say.

"Sixteen! Miss Bill, what are you doing, bringing a minor to audition for me? I could lose my license if

I put her on stage during cabaret hours!"

"You were her age the first time you performed in a bar," Miss Bill says.

"That was the eighties," Abundance says. "We didn't have cameras on our phones! Our phones didn't even leave the house!"

"So that's it?" I say. "It's over?"

"Wait!" Miss Bill says. "Why don't you let her host her own show for queens her age before cabaret hours."

"Like an all-ages drag show?" Abundance asks.

"Sure! Whatever you want to call it," Miss Bill says.

"I have been looking for a way to pick up business on Tuesday evenings," Abundance says. "How about this? I'll let you and all your little social media friends do a show from seven to nine p.m. on Tuesdays. You do all the promoting and I'll give you a third of the door."

"*All* of the door!" Miss Bill says.

"I won't be making money on booze," Abundance says.

"Eighty/Twenty," Miss Bill counters.

"Seventy/Thirty," Abundance counter-counters.

"Done!" Miss Bill says and they shake hands. "We'll see you in two weeks."

Miss Bill ushers me out the door before Abundance has a chance to change her mind.

"I don't know the first thing about putting on a drag show," I whisper.

"No one does the first time they do it," Miss Bill whispers back.

18 Trouble in Paradise

I'M SOAKING IN THE TUB with a face mask. My feet are killing me from my audition at Poodles. I'll put some ice on them when I get out of the tub. There's a knock on the apartment door. I close my eyes and take in the day. I hear Mom talking to someone in the living room. I wonder who it could be.

"Joshua," Mom says through the door. "Ivan is here to see you."

I sit up in the tub so fast that water sloshes over

the side.

"Joshua? Are you okay?" Mom asks.

"I need a minute," I say.

I hop out of the tub and wrap a towel around myself. I check my face in the mirror. The Amy make-up is all gone except for some eyeliner. There's no time for that now. I need to get out there before Mom blows my cover. I find Ivan on the couch with my mother. He looks overwhelmed.

"And when I told her I knew she was seeing my husband behind my back, do you know what That Bitch Becky said?" Mom says to Ivan, pausing like she's about to drop a bombshell. "She said, 'I don't know what you're talking about.'"

"Hi, Ivan," I say, dripping water all over the living room floor. "Why didn't you call to say you were coming over?"

"I did," he says. "But you didn't pick up."

"I left my phone in my room while I was taking my bath," I say. "Mom, is it okay if Ivan and I talk alone in my room?"

"Of course," Mom says. "No sex!"

"Scout's honour," Ivan says, crossing his heart as he gets up from the couch.

"You never said you were a Boy Scout," I say as we walk to my room.

"I wasn't," Ivan says. "I was just really uncomfortable listening to your mom talk about her love life."

I open the door and see Amy Winehouse's hair and dress lying on the floor. I stop so fast Ivan runs into me. I grab the towel to keep it from falling off.

"Do you mind waiting outside a second while I get dressed?" I ask.

"Sure thing," Ivan says. "Take your time."

I shut the door and shove my wig, dress and heels as quickly and carefully as I can into the closet. Then I scramble for something decent to wear. My hands are shaking. What if he's here to break up with me? If he is, I want to look my best to make it as hard as possible for him.

"Ta dah!" I say, opening the door for him wearing a pair of jeans and a T-shirt.

Ivan steps into the room I share with Ed and looks around.

"Bunk beds," he says. "Cool!"

"I guess. Ed snores so loud sometimes I can feel it through the mattress."

"That sounds like Ed, all right."

"Want to sit down?" I ask, taking a seat on the bottom bunk. Ivan sits next to me, to my surprise. There is a small distance between us that does not bode well.

"Are you okay?" Ivan asks. "Your eyes look sunken in."

That would be the eyeliner.

"I haven't been sleeping well since our date at the ice rink," I say.

"I wanted to apologize for that," he says. "You were right. The guys were being idiots. I tend to double down when people call me out on my crap."

"I'm sorry for storming off the ice," I say. "I can be a little over-the-top sometimes."

"A little?"

"I'm not above taking back my apology," I say.

"I was kidding," Ivan says. He puts his hand on my knee. I breathe a sigh of relief. I was worried I would never feel his touch again. "But if this is going to work, then you're going to need to accept that I enjoy being 'one of the guys' every now and then."

"Being 'one of the guys' is okay as long as you're not toxic when you do it," I say.

"I promise," Ivan says. "But I'm bound to screw up again. It's what I fall back to when I'm around straight guys. I recognize it now, though."

"I'm willing to be patient while you learn to be the gay hockey type, if you can accept that I'm gay AF. I couldn't pass for straight if I did steroids and bench pressed a smart car."

"You looked butch when you changed the tire on my car," Ivan says, nudging me with his elbow. I nudge him back. He skootches over on the bed and presses his leg against mine. He puts his arm around me and I rest my head on his shoulder.

"Did we just make up?" I ask.

"Not yet." Ivan kisses me softly on the lips. "Now we did. Want to make out?"

"You literally just crossed your heart and told my mom you wouldn't have sex with me."

"I'm not a Boy Scout," Ivan says. "And making out isn't sex."

"Okay, just not on Ed's bed. He'll be so grossed out," I say.

We scramble up to the top bunk and lie down facing each other. Ivan kisses my face, giggling.

"I feel like a kid at camp," he says.

"What camp did you go to?" I ask. I blink and my left eyelid is stuck closed. I must not have got all the eyelash glue off my eyes.

"What's wrong with your eyelid?" Ivan says.

"Birth defect," I say, pulling my eyelid open with my fingers and go back to kissing him.

"So why didn't you answer my call this afternoon?" Ivan says. "I expected you to play hard-to-get. I didn't expect you to ghost me."

"I was helping Miss Bill," I say. "He can be

really nosy."

"Why do you call him Miss Bill?"

"Because he's a diva."

"That is one way of describing him," Ivan says.

There's disdain in Ivan's voice. I'm taken by surprise. I never suspected Ivan had a problem with Miss Bill. Before I can give it another thought, Ivan pulls me closer to him and we start making out again.

19 Planet Claire

ME, MISS BILL, KARA AND CHRIS are sitting in the dance studio Miss Bill's friend is letting us use for drag-show auditions. According to Miss Bill, his friend also uses the studio to teach nude yoga. I'm making a point of not touching the floor with my hands.

The show is less than a week away. Kara and Chris have been helping me cast as wide a net as possible. We want to attract as many aspiring drag queens and kings as we can find. We've created a Facebook page,

Instagram posters and TikTok videos. We even made paper fliers and posted them in coffee shops. I was expecting to be fighting queens off with a stick, based on the number of Look Queens on social media. But the audition starts in five minutes and no one is here.

"This isn't good," I say, my voice echoing in the empty studio.

"Give it a minute," Miss Bill says. "This is what is known as Drag Time."

The words are barely out of his mouth when two blonde queens stumble into the studio. They look lost and unsure. Both of them are wearing long coats and carrying large bags. I can't tell if this how they dress every day or a look they put together for the audition.

"Are you here to audition for the drag show?" I say jovially.

"This *is* the place," one of the blondes lisps. "I was sure we were being sold into slavery."

"That would explain the disappointing turnout," Chris mutters.

"Are you two here together?" I ask.

"We met on the stairs," the other blonde says. "I'm Claire from Tech Support."

"Oh?" Miss Bill says. "We don't have a computer here."

"No, that's my drag name," Claire says.

"I'm UFOria," says the other queen. "As in U-F-O-ria."

"Charmed, I'm sure," Miss Bill says, a little baffled.

"I'm Josh, I'm the emcee," I say. "This is my drag mother, Miss Bill. And that's Kara and Chris. They're helping out with the show."

"Nice to meet you," UFOria says.

"Shall we get started?" I say. "Who wants to go first?"

"I don't mind going first," says Claire.

Claire whips off her coat, revealing a silver mini-dress. She opens her bag and pulls out a shake-and-go wig and some heels, then she uses her phone as a mirror to put on some lipstick. Claire performs "Juice" by Lizzo. Her dress is dazzling as she struts around the studio. I'm kind of jealous of how easy she makes it look.

UFOria strips down to a flesh-toned body suit that's been beaded to cover her private parts. She slips a pair of silicone boobs into her suit and throws on a wig that comes down to her butt.

"My ass is usually bigger," UFOria says. "But the last time I wore pads on the bus I was harassed by every dirty old man in Vancouver."

"We're everywhere," Miss Bill says.

"Right?" says UFOria.

"I think the hair dye has seeped into her brain," Miss Bill whispers.

UFOria performs "Womanizer" by Britney Spears. Her number, like her costume, borders on porn. She humps everything in the studio, the barre, the mirror, the floor and even Miss Bill. I notice that even Kara is turned on by her act. UFOria finishes the number by kicking her leg out and falling forward in a death drop, her other leg bent behind her on the floor.

"What did you think?" UFOria asks us, as she struggles to a seated position.

"That I could use a cold shower," Miss Bill says.

"What's that supposed to mean?" UFOria asks.

"It was great," I say.

"Does that mean we're in the show?" Claire asks.

"Yes, it does," Miss Bill says. "Give Kara your phone number and we'll let you know when to be at the show. Prepare two numbers."

Claire and UFOria jump for joy and hug each other. Then they gather their things and leave. We have the studio for another ninety minutes and no other queens have shown up to audition.

"What are we going to do?" I ask. "We can't do a drag show with only three queens."

"You're right," Chris says. "This show needs a drag king. I volunteer Kara."

"Oh, hell, no," she says. "I'm not getting on that stage."

"Chris is right," Miss Bill says to Kara. "A drag king is exactly what the show needs."

"I am not going to be your token drag king," Kara says, waving him off. "Besides, I don't know the first thing about doing serious drag."

"You'll probably get a date out of it," Miss Bill says.

"Where do you want me to stand?" Kara asks.

Miss Bill spends the next hour helping Kara perform as a drag king. She's a natural performer. If I didn't know she was a girl, I would ask her out. Once Kara feels she has the hang of things, Miss Bill spends some time helping me out with the songs I plan to perform for the show. Everyone is having a good time, experimenting with our performances.

"You know, Claire reminds me of this great song from the eighties. Have you ever heard of a band called the B-52s?" Miss Bill says. "I have a great idea for a duet."

"I'm game," Kara says.

"Me, too," I say.

My phone starts vibrating in my pocket. It's Ivan. I answer the phone panting, out of breath from all the dancing I've been doing.

"Are you panting or just happy to hear from me?" Ivan asks.

"A bit of both," I tell him. "I'm horsing around with Miss Bill and the Wonder Twins."

"Again?"

"What's that supposed to mean?"

"You seem to spend a lot of time with him."

"Is that a problem?"

"It's cool," Ivan says. "I got off work early and wanted to see if you were into hanging out."

I watch Miss Bill showing Kara and Chris some old dance moves. They're smiling and having the time of their lives.

"I think I'm good," I tell him. "Why don't I give you a call when I get home."

20 Video Games

IVAN AND I ARE SITTING on his bed shooting zombies on his TV. I'm not a fan of first-person shooter games. I'm only doing this to make up for the all the time with him I've missed, rehearsing and organizing the show. I'm hoping that doing things Ivan enjoys will soften the blow when I tell him about Siri Alexa and the drag show.

The show is all I can think about, even while shooting zombies. We open in less than a week. Kara,

Chris and I have been promoting the hell out of it. We've received some pretty nasty messages online from religious wingnuts accusing us of being child molesters. I know that they're only trolls, but it hurts all the same.

Kara and I have been working on our duet with Miss Bill in our spare time. Miss Bill has been helping me write jokes to use as witty banter while I emcee the show. I'm exhausted. I'm also the happiest I've ever been. This is all I ever wanted.

"So, what have you been up to lately?" Ivan asks. "I feel like we never see each other anymore."

I could tell Ivan the truth. Just pour my soul out to him. I could even perform "Rehab" for him. But it feels so cozy here in his room, even if it takes shooting zombies. This is exactly what I imagined having a boyfriend would be like. But never with someone who looked like Ivan. He pauses the game and puts down his controller.

"If I ask you something, do you promise to give me an honest answer?" he says.

This is it. He found out I do drag. Ed must have told him. Or maybe he saw one of the posters for the show.

"Are you cheating on me?" he asks.

I laugh out loud. Maybe too loud.

"Of course not," I say. "What makes you think that?"

"You've been so unavailable lately," he says.

"I have school and homework. Plus, I'm trying to earn some extra cash with delivery. And I've been spending a little more time with Miss Bill lately."

"If you like Miss Bill so much, why don't you marry him?"

"That's mature."

"I still don't get what you see in that old queen. What does he have to offer that I don't?"

"He tells stories about being gay in the sixties and seventies. He's exposed me to movies and music I never would have found on my own. And he makes me appreciate what I have as a gay guy."

"But he's so over the top," Ivan moans. "The clothes,

the limp wrist. Acting like a queen. It's so outdated."

"That's who he is."

"Guys like him make it hard for rest of us. It's no wonder those right-wing nuts in the government think we're coming for their children."

"Don't blame homophobia on drag queens. Drag queens are responsible for the rights we enjoy today."

"I know, I know . . . Drag queens were the first ones to fight back at Stonewall."

"Not just Stonewall. Drag queens like Bill raised thousands of dollars for the AIDS research that gave us PReP. We owe people like Bill our lives."

"Can we agree to disagree about this?"

"We need to talk about this," I say. "I'm not that much different from Bill. Do I embarrass you?"

"Of course not!"

"Then why are you holding Bill to a higher standard?"

Ivan rolls his eyes like he wishes he hadn't opened his big mouth. The feeling is mutual.

"I think it's offensive, okay?" he says. "No one

needs to act that gay in this day and age."

Wow. As much as I was afraid to tell Ivan that I do drag, deep down I always thought he would be cool with it. I should tell him now. But what difference does it make? I don't know if I want to date someone who would say Miss Bill *offends* him. I'm not even sure I could be friends with him. This can't be how he really feels. And I don't want to discuss it in the state I'm in right now. I might say something I regret.

"I should go," I say.

"Come on, Josh. You can't keep leaving every time we have a disagreement."

"That's not why I'm leaving."

"Miss Bill isn't my cup of tea, that's all. Just like my friends from work aren't yours."

"But in some circles, your friends' behaviour is acceptable. It's even encouraged. Whereas Miss Bill is ridiculed for who he is, even by other gay people."

"You're blowing this out of proportion."

"This may come as a surprise, but I actually butch it up for you when we hang out. Sometimes to the point I worry I'm sacrificing a piece of myself. And I'm not sure you notice."

"I notice."

"You don't act like it," I say. "I'll call you tomorrow."

I say a quick hello to my mom when I come home from Ivan's. The lights are off in our room except for the glow of Ed's laptop coming from the bottom bunk.

"Please tell me you're not watching porn," I say, climbing up to my bed.

"It's the 2010 Olympic gold medal hockey game," Ed says. "What's wrong? Did you break a heel?"

"Don't even joke about that," I say. I hang my head over the side of my mattress and ask Ed, "Why are guys such jerks?"

"You're a guy. Don't you know?"

"Why are we so hung up on being one of the guys? Why can't we be vulnerable once in a while?"

"It's a sign of weakness."

"Have you told Ivan I do drag?"

"You asked me not to, so I didn't," he says. "Ivan still doesn't know?"

"I'm afraid he'll break up with me if I tell him."

"Dude, he'll break up with you if you don't."

It's the first piece of sound advice my brother has ever given me. And it might already be too late.

21 Five Stars

THE DELIVERY APP displays Ivan's address. It's the exact same order as the first time I delivered food to his house. I wonder if he's deliberately trying to get me to come over or if it's just a happy coincidence. Maybe it's the Goddess's way of telling me to grow up and face my fears. I accept the order.

Ivan and I haven't talked in a couple of days, except for some non-committal texts. I want to talk to him. But I don't know what to say. I'm worried he's going to say something so offensive that I'll *have* to break up with him. I'm also afraid that he's not willing to put up with all my drama. I never expected our relationship to last forever. But I never saw it ending this soon.

You're projecting, Kara would say if she could hear my thoughts.

I take a deep breath before I ring the doorbell. I could be working myself up over nothing. The order might not even be for Ivan. It could be for his parents. The door opens. It's Ivan.

"If you wanted to talk to me, you could have just called," I joke.

"No, I was hungry," he says.

Why don't you just kick me in the gut while you're at it, Ivan.

"Want to come in?" he asks.

"Sure," I say. "Let me sign off the app."

We sit next to each other at the kitchen island. He pulls his food out of the bag and starts eating without offering me any.

"So are things okay between us?" he asks.

"They could be better," I say.

"How?"

"You could stop being such a hater when it comes to Miss Bill."

"I don't hate the guy. I barely know him."

"Then why does his femininity offend you?"

"I like sports and video games. When I was a kid, I preferred playing with WWE action figures over Barbie dolls. That's just who I am."

"We all played with WWE action figures. They were sex dolls for pre-teen gay boys. The problem is that you can't accept the guys who played with Barbie."

"I accept you. You're effeminate."

"After I beat you at hockey and changed your tire."

"That *was* kind of sexy."

We both laugh at his attempt to defuse the situation. It's the first time I've felt like we're a couple since the argument.

"You're missing the point, Ivan. I'm gay AF. But I can do all the things 'boys' are supposed to do. So doesn't that make me masculine?"

"But you're not like Miss Bill. He takes things to the extreme. He makes such a show of being gay."

"That doesn't mean he's not masculine. He's just not *your* idea of masculine."

"You're comparing apples to oranges."

"Ivan, I'm a drag queen."

I experience the same feeling of relief as when I told my parents I was gay. The news came as a shock to no one, but I needed to hear myself say the words to them out loud. Now comes the hard part. Confronting how Ivan feels about speaking my truth.

"You're only saying that to prove your point."

"I'm saying it because it's true. The reason I haven't been spending as much time with you lately is that I'm putting on a drag show. It's my debut in front of a live audience. Here, look."

I pull out my phone and show him Siri Alexa's Instagram page. He scrolls through the photos, not believing me at first. He looks at my face and compares it against the photos in my stream.

"That was you at the Dugout when I went on that date with Randall."

"It was."

"I looked right at you and you pretended not to know me."

"I was in disguise. And not a bad one, if I say so myself."

"You were spying on me!"

"I was worried you and Randall would hit it off."

"You were the one who said I should go on the date in the first place."

"I wanted you to be sure that I was the person you wanted to be with."

"So, you were testing me?"

"No! I was worried you were only dating me out of pity."

"Jiminy Crickets, Josh! I don't remember ordering a side of drama with my lunch."

"It came free with purchase," I try to joke.

Ivan doesn't think it's funny. "It feels like you've been lying to me these last few weeks," he says. "It's like you didn't trust me at all. Not with Randall, not with your drag."

"So, you do have a problem with me doing drag?"

"I'm not thrilled about it. But it probably wouldn't have been a deal breaker."

"'Wouldn't have been'? As in the past tense? So, you're breaking up with me?"

"It feels pretty mutual to me. Me not liking Miss Bill is a deal breaker for you. And your lack of faith in me is a giant red flag from where I'm sitting. Can we really keep going on like this?"

"I guess not," I say, wishing I could rewind the last few minutes. "I guess I'll be going. I hope you'll still give me five stars on the app."

I slink out of Ivan's house and head back home. Instead of going back to the apartment, I knock on Miss Bill's door on my way up. He's dressed in his black silk pajamas and has an ascot around his neck. He looks like he's dressed for a cocktail party, even though he's home alone. On the bike ride home, I wondered if I hadn't hitched my wagon to the wrong star when I sided with Miss Bill. Looking at him now, I can see what my future could look like. It's not so bad. In fact, it's pretty fabulous.

"What's got you down?" Miss Bill asks.

"Ivan and I broke up," I say.

"Why?"

"Among other things, you offend him."

"Where does he live? I want to throw a drink in his face."

I know Miss Bill is only putting on a show. But it's the show I need right now.

22 Heel Malfunction

I FOCUS ON THE SHOW to take my mind off Ivan. Not only am I performing, I'm also the emcee. I'm more nervous about coming up with witty banter than I am about my lip-sync. Miss Bill gave me a few old jokes from his act. They seem kind of dated and not what I would call "woke."

I have the apartment to myself. I might as well kill two birds with one stone and vacuum the apartment in my heels while I rehearse. I use the vacuum handle as a microphone to get used to talking with one in my hand. I'm going over the joke about the gay guy who gets kidnapped by a herd of gorillas. The good thing about old jokes is that no one my age has heard them.

"Did it hurt?" I say to my imaginary audience. "'Did it *hurt?*' the gay guy said. 'He never writes, he never calls . . .'"

That's when I trip over the vacuum cord. I fall over and bang my leg on the coffee table. The vacuum cleaner lands on top of me. I lie there on the floor, glad that no one is around to record this with their phone. Then the pain sets in. It shoots up from my foot into my knee like someone is pounding my ankle with a spike. I try to get up. I can't put any weight on my foot.

I crawl onto the couch and try to adjust to the pain. I try to stand up again and fall right back onto the couch. I hop on one foot to the bathroom to get Ed's tensor bandage and wind it around my ankle. Then I pop an anti-inflammatory pill and go to get the ice pack from the freezer.

I think I might have done some serious damage. I need to go to the emergency room. Mom will panic if I tell her I need to go to the hospital. I call Kara and it goes straight to voicemail. Same with Chris. An ambulance is out of the question. I swallow my pride and call Ivan. I'm surprised when he picks up.

"Would you mind taking me to the Emergency Room?"

"I'll be right there," Ivan says.

Ivan is at my place in less than fifteen minutes. He actually carries me in his arms from the apartment to his car. What was I thinking when I was so hard on him last week? No one does this kind of thing.

There are only a handful of people waiting in the Emergency Room. The intake nurse says it won't be long for the doctor to see me.

"Seeing anyone special?" I ask as a joke.

"I've been hanging out with Randall a bit," Ivan says, like he's telling me the weather.

"Pause and rewind! Did you say you've been seeing Randall?"

"He called as soon as he found out we broke up."

"And how did he find that out?"

"Ed told him."

"I thought you didn't hit it off with him," I remind him.

"He's okay. When he's not talking about the gym. Or himself."

"He only wants to get down your pants," I say. "The moment he does he'll move on to the next person."

"Thank you for being happy for me," Ivan says.

"I'm not happy for you," I say.

"I thought a drag queen would know sarcasm when she heard it."

"Joshua?" The Emergency Room doctor is looking around the waiting room for me.

I wince as I get up on my good foot. Ivan puts my arm around his shoulder, supporting me as I limp to the Emergency Room bed. The doctor examines my ankle. He squeezes it in places. I yelp in pain. He asks me to wiggle my toes.

"It's not broken," the doctor says. "I'll do some X-rays to make sure. In any case, you're going to have to stay off it for a few days and let it heal."

"But I'm hosting my first drag show in forty-eight hours."

"You can still host the show," the doctor says. "As long as you do it sitting down. If you put too much pressure on that ankle, it's never going to heal."

"I can't believe this is happening," I say.

"Let your boyfriend be your servant for a few days," the doctor says.

"We're not boyfriends," we both say at the same time.

"You could have fooled me, with the way you were bickering in the waiting room."

It takes another hour to be discharged from the hospital. Ivan and I are mostly silent. I get that we're broken up. But I didn't expect him to start dating so soon. Especially Randall. He might as well date one of his WWE action figures. They have more personality.

The doctor gives me a pair of crutches. I'm able to

limp back to Ivan's car without his assistance, although I crave being close to him again. Ivan helps me get comfortable in the front seat. It reminds me of the time Mom drove me to my first day of kindergarten, the way he's so careful about it.

"I'm sorry you have to miss your drag show," Ivan says.

"Thanks," I say.

"I would have gone if you asked me," he says.

"That's nice of you say."

"I mean it, Josh. I had a lot of fun being your boyfriend. If there's anything I can do to make you feel better, just let me know."

"You could stop seeing Randall."

"I meant for your ankle."

"So did I," I say.

It was worth a try. I know Ivan is trying to make me feel better. But he's only making my heart ache more. Why couldn't he be as understanding about Miss Bill as he is about my ankle?

23 Man with a Plan

KARA'S JAW DROPS when I show up to school on crutches. I was too tired and hopped up on painkillers to return the fifty million texts she sent asking how I was doing. Plus, after the night I had, I could use a good "reveal."

"Holy crap, Joshua!" she says. "Is it broken?"

"Sprained," I say.

Randall walks toward us in the hall, all high and mighty, with his nose in the air. I wonder if Ivan has told him about our night at the ER. Randall sees the crutches under my armpits and laughs.

"Break a heel, Joshua?" he asks.

"As a matter of fact, I did, Randall," I shout back at him. I hear him laugh all the way down to the end of the hall. I feel like a bigger loser than when I hobbled into school.

"Please tell me you weren't doing a death drop," Kara says. "You know how I feel about death drops."

"I tripped while vacuuming the apartment in my heels. I could have died."

"Could you imagine if you died vacuuming the apartment in heels?" Chris says. "No one would be able to sit through your funeral with a straight face."

"You could be a doctor with that bedside manner," I tell Chris. I turn to Kara. "I think you're going to have to host the show for me."

"I can't do that," she says. "The only time I speak in class is when the teacher calls on me."

"Do you think I want to bail on the show?" I ask. "This is my baby."

"I recommend finding some wicked painkillers," Chris says. "I can think of at least ten rich kids in this school who steal pills from their parents' medicine cabinets."

"I have painkillers," I tell him.

"I'm talking rich-kid painkillers," Chris says.

"The last thing I need is to be hopped up on pills for my drag debut," I say.

"But it will look so good on your Wikipedia page after you're dead," Chris says.

"Do we have to decide now?" Kara asks. "You still have a day. Ice the hell out of it and see what happens."

"Okay," I tell her. "But be prepared to go on in my place if I can't do it."

The school day is torture. My ankle is throbbing by the end of the day. When I get home, Ed lets me use the bottom bunk to rest and ice my ankle. There's a knock on my bedroom door. Miss Bill pokes his head inside my room.

"Joshua?" he whispers.

I stick my hand out from under the top bunk and wave. Miss Bill enters the room, looking around like a chicken in a slaughterhouse.

"I haven't been in contact with this much testosterone since gym class in 1957," he says. "How are you, darling?"

"I wish I was dead," I pout.

"Still performing for the back row, I see. You can't be all that bad, then."

"I'm thinking about letting Kara emcee the show for me."

"You poured your blood, sweat and tears into that show. You can't give up now."

"Now you're the one who's overreacting."

"Don't ever diminish your effort, Joshua. You're doing something incredible. How many queens your age put on a drag show?"

"None."

"See? You're a trailblazer."

"I had a good drag mother."

"I love it when you lie," Miss Bill says.

There's another knock on the door. Ivan steps into the room. The sight of his face makes me feel a hundred times better. I want to get out of bed and kiss him. Miss Bill *humphs* when he sees Ivan. Ivan looks everywhere around the room except at Miss Bill.

"Is it me or did the temperature drop?" Miss Bill says. He makes a great show of giving me a peck on the cheek. "Now you get some rest and don't you dare think about not being in that show."

Miss Bill raises his nose in the air, throws his invisible scarf over his shoulder and exits stage left. Ivan sees me stretched out on Ed's bed with two big bags of ice on my ankle.

"You look like crap," he says.

"Flattery will get you nowhere," I tell him. "Shouldn't you be at the gym, spotting Randall?"

"I'm here to help," he says. "Wait here."

"Where would I go?"

Ivan sighs. He leaves the room and comes back a moment later with a dolly, the kind you use for moving furniture. Ivan parks the dolly in front of my

WALK THIS WAY

bed and leans against it.

"Get on," he says.

"Are you going to push me down the stairs?"

"I'm going to push you around the stage while you do drag."

"I'm not getting on that thing. I'll break my neck *and* my ankle."

"Trust me, I've moved heavier stuff than you with this thing."

There's something about the way he says 'trust me' that gives me the confidence to give it a try. Ivan helps me up onto the dolly. I hang onto the sides real tight, then he leans the dolly back and pushes me through the bedroom door. I scream like a girl.

"Relax your shoulders into my chest," he says.

I do as I'm told. I can feel his pecs against my shoulder blades. It reminds me of the times we used to cuddle on his bed and watch TV. I don't know if I can go through with this. I love being this close to him. But it's killing me.

"What the hell?" Ed says when he sees us.

Ivan pushes me around the living room while I lip-sync to "Rehab" for Ed. Ed falls back onto the couch like he's seen everything.

"Mom," Ed shouts into the kitchen. "Joshy's doing drag on a dolly."

24 Bumper to Bumper

IT'S OPENING NIGHT. I check myself in the mirror one last time. My stomach is rumbling and my hands are shaking. I've agreed to let Ivan drive me to the show. Kara thinks I'm nuts. Chris thinks I'm secretly trying to get Ivan back. They're both right.

Mom and Ed are already on their way to Poodles to get a good seat. Seeing Ed at a gay bar will be worth all the effort I put into the show. This is the first time my family is coming to cheer me on. It's always been about Ed and his hockey games in the past. I hope I don't let them down.

The intercom buzzes and I let Ivan into the building. I open the apartment door and he shoves a small bouquet of flowers into my chest, nearly knocking me off my crutches.

"For you," he says.

He puts the flowers in some water for me and then carries me down the stairs. I feel like a princess. A princess with a beehive, temporary tattoos and Egyptian eyeliner. Would Ivan be doing all of this if he didn't still have feelings for me?

We get in the car and I go through the checklist of things I need before we leave. The car is not even at the end of the block when Ivan says, "I invited Randall. I hope you don't mind."

"I would punch you but I don't want to break a nail," I say. "What makes you think it would be okay to bring Randall?"

"He wanted to come. What was I going to say? No?"

"Yes. That's exactly what you say. The only reason he's coming is to rub it in that you two are dating."

"I'll make sure he doesn't sit close to the stage."

"Oh, he'll just love that," I say. We merge onto the Trans-Canada Highway. The traffic is already backed up. "Of course, it's bumper-to-bumper traffic. We're going to be late. I should have gone with Mom and Ed."

"Bro, I'm going to get you there on time," Ivan says. "And I never said Randall and I are dating. We're *seeing* each other. There's a difference."

I don't know if Ivan is just saying that to calm me down. But it works. Tonight could be my chance to get him back. And in drag, no less. That would really piss off Randall.

There's a crowd in front of Poodles when we get there. It looks like every queer kid, freak and teenage girl is lined up on the sidewalk to get into the cabaret.

"Holy crap!" I say. "People actually came!"

"Of course!" Ivan says.

I get out of the car. I'm about to hobble into Poodles on my crutches. Ivan runs around to the other side with the dolly.

"Your chariot awaits," he says.

"You've been waiting to say that all day, haven't you?"

"Yes," he says.

The doorman looks astonished when he sees me being rolled in on the dolly.

"And who do you think you are?" he asks.

"The star of this show," I say, as we glide past.

Ivan pushes me backstage where Miss Bill, Kara, Claire and UFOria are waiting for me. Abundance O'Caution pokes her head backstage to see how we're doing. She notices that I'm on a dolly with a bandage around my ankle.

"Heel malfunction?" Abundance asks. I nod yes. "I hate when that happens. Show starts in five minutes."

"Are you seriously going out on that thing?" Kara asks.

"I think it's genius," Miss Bill says. "Very camp."

"It was Ivan's idea," I tell him.

"My opinion of you might be changing," Miss Bill says to Ivan. He stands in front of me and stuffs a kerchief inside my bra. "For luck. And to wipe the sweat out of your eyes. It gets hot under those lights."

"Thanks for everything," I say.

"Who would think when I told you to turn your music down all those weeks ago that we would end up here," he says. "I'm going to take my seat before I ruin my facelift. Break a leg, everyone. Except for Joshua, he's in rough shape as it is."

Me and my three drag performers, plus Ivan, stand backstage looking at each other expectantly. My heart is racing.

"I can't believe we're actually doing this!" Kara squeals.

I hear Abundance come onto the stage and tap the mic to make sure that it's on. "Ladies, gentlemen and everyone in between," he says with his performer's voice. "Welcome to Poodles for the first ever License to Drag

Show, with an incredible cast of underage performers. And now, your host for the evening, Siri Alexa!"

Ivan tilts me back in the dolly and pushes me through the curtains onto the stage. I feel like I'm plunging down a waterslide for the very first time. The audience gasps when they see me and then starts applauding.

"Excuse the dolly, everyone," I say to the crowd. "This is what happens when you have zero stars on Uber."

To my amazement, the audience laughs. I look out across the crowd. Mom and Ed are sitting at the table closest to the stage with Miss Bill and Chris. Then I see Randall with some of the jocks from school. He has a smarmy look on his face like he can't wait to see me fail.

The joke is on him. This isn't the Dugout. We're on my turf now. And I'm about to mop the floor with his bubble butt.

25 Take a Bow

I CAN'T BELIEVE THE LOVE the audience is showering on us. Some of the jokes I wrote are getting bigger laughs than they deserve. I don't care. I'm loving the attention.

We take a fifteen-minute break to let people get drinks and mingle. I go out into the crowd on my crutches to look for Mom and Miss Bill. I'm stopped by at least five Look Queens from IG who want to be in the next show. I'm tempted to be a diva and throw them shade. Where were they for the audition? But I refuse to be one of those bitchy queens. I want this show to be a venue where queens my age can develop their act in real life. I tell each of them to DM me and we'll take it from there.

"Joshua!" Mom says, giving me a hug from behind that nearly pushes me over. She's tipsy. It's actually kind of refreshing to see her this relaxed for a change. "I'm so proud of you. If I had known vacuuming the apartment in heels would lead to this, I would have had you do it ages ago."

"Mom, stop leaning on Joshy," Ed says getting her off me. "You're going to sprain his other ankle."

"Thanks, Ed," I say. "Keep an eye on her, will you?"

"Will do, little buddy," Ed says. Then he does something we haven't done since we were kids. He hugs me. "Congratulations, Bro."

I look around the cabaret for Miss Bill. I don't see him anywhere. I run into Chris and Kara instead.

"Oh, my god!" Kara says. "I can't believe how much fun I'm having!"

"She is a total dyke magnet right now," Chris says. "I'm kind of jealous."

"I might actually lose my virginity before I graduate high school," she says.

"I'm sure Grandma will be excited to hear all about it," Chris says.

"Have you seen Miss Bill?" I finally ask, still looking around the cabaret. Chris taps the shoulder behind him. Miss Bill spins around like a dancer.

"There you are!" Miss Bill says, air-kissing each side of my face. "The show is fabulous!"

"Do you really think so?"

"I'll be amazed if you don't walk out of here with a couple of hundred bucks in your purse," he says. "Then you can buy *me* some heels."

"I think Ivan is getting used to seeing me as a drag queen," I say. "I'm going to ask him if he wants to get back together after the show."

"Do you think that's a good idea?"

"I know he said some bad things about you. But Ivan is a good guy. He'll come around."

"That's not what I mean," he says.

Miss Bill steps aside and I see Ivan and Randall leaning against the bar. Randall is staring into Ivan's eyes like he's under Ivan's control. Ivan is smiling back at him. They are the picture of happiness. Randall stands on his tiptoes and kisses Ivan on the forehead. I don't have time to process what I'm watching before Abundance O'Caution taps me on the shoulder and says, "You're on in five minutes."

"Are you going to be okay?" Miss Bill says. "Do you want a hand getting backstage?"

"I'm okay," I say.

Ivan catches up with me as I'm about to go through the beaded curtains.

"Here, let me help you," he says.

"I can take it from here," I tell him.

"Don't you want the dolly?"

"I'm feeling pretty good. Why don't you take a seat and enjoy the rest of the show?"

"I don't mind. I'm having fun."

"You've been a big help already. It means a lot to me."

"Any time, Joshua."

I watch Ivan walk to where Randall is hanging out at the bar. I have one chance to get Ivan back. I better not blow it. I hobble back onto the stage with my crutches and get the audience's attention.

"Welcome back, everyone!" I say into the mic. "Let's start things off with a song that's near and dear to my heart. This one goes out to Ivan. It's called 'Back to Black.'"

I can see Ivan's face beaming from the back of the bar. Randall is scowling at me. He's onto me. Let him scowl all he wants.

I go back to the little jazz bar in my mind. This time the only person in the room is Ivan. Amy Winehouse wrote the song after her boyfriend left her to go back to his ex. It's a song about returning to the life you had before you were with the one you love, which is exactly how I feel. I pour out my soul to Ivan through Amy's lyrics. I lean on one of my crutches like it's a mic stand. The crowd litters the stage with five- and ten-dollar bills. But all I see is

Ivan's eyes staring back at me until the song ends.

We end the show with the number Miss Bill showed Kara and me the day of the audition, "Planet Claire" by the B-52s. After we take our final bows, I go outside for some air and to catch my breath. I'm afraid to go back inside to see Ivan with Randall.

"Did someone call an Uber?"

I turn around, and there's Ivan, posing with the dolly.

"Shouldn't you be measuring Randall's biceps?"

"About Randall," Ivan says. "I was thinking I might have ended things between us too soon."

"I was kind of regretting not fighting for what we had, myself."

"We had a good thing going," Ivan says. "I've learned a lot about myself being with you."

"Same."

"I'm not a drag queen. But I had a lot of fun with you on stage tonight."

"Guys are always saying they're not a drag queen before they put on a dress."

"Not this again," Ivan says, elbowing me shyly.

"Yes, this again," I say, elbowing him back.

"I bought Miss Bill a drink," Ivan says.

"You're not old enough to get served."

"I'm cute, Josh. Even I know that."

"You're trouble, is what you are," I say. "Did Miss Bill throw the drink in your face?"

"He said he would have but he didn't want to waste perfectly good alcohol," Ivan says. "Then he told me to go find you."

"And here I am."

"So, what do you say, Siri Alexa? Another round on the dolly?"

"What about Randall?"

"I told him he could hang out. But that I'm taking you home. Randall is hot, but he's not as much fun as you."

"That's what I've been saying this whole time."

Ivan grabs the dolly and says, "Your chariot awaits."

"I hate to see what it turns back into at midnight,"

I say, as I get on. Ivan tilts the dolly back and gives me a kiss on the lips. And then he wheels me off into the sunset. Or in this case, Poodles.

Acknowledgements

Thank you, Kat Mototsune, for all your help developing this story. I am grateful for your patience and understanding while I tried to navigate Joshua's journey from Look Queen to Drag Queen. It's been such a pleasure working with you these last few years. I would also like to thank the team at Lorimer for getting this novel and my previous three novels off my hard drive and into the hands of readers.

To my friends Billeh Nickerson, Mette Bach and Dean Mirau, thank you for having more faith in my talents than I do. To Mark Vossberg, thank you for answering all my pesky drag questions and for teaching me the secret to learning to walk in high heels. And to Kendall Gender, thank you for bringing me up to speed on today's drag scene.

This novel was written over the course of six months at the height of the COVID-19 pandemic and during a period of personal challenges. I would like to honour those I lost during the writing of this book: my sister, Maria Arruda; my brother, Joe Correia and my friend, Chuck Davis, who taught me how to mix and enjoy a dirty martini.

Lastly, I would like to thank Bill Monroe, to whom this book is dedicated. You were mentor to me in my twenties and now you are showing me how to age gracefully, and with dignity, in middle age. During these trying times, it always helped to hear you say, "The only thing constant is change."